Return to Grymballia

To Judy —
With love ♡
Pat McCaw

Pat McCaw

Dedicated to
the Back Row
Ninjas.

Chapter 1

I leaped out of the portal and stepped out of the cave – "Grymballia, I'm back!"

What happened? Beautiful Grymballia was dark and gray. My stomach turned. The forest was silent without songs drifting through the trees, and the sky contained neither birds nor sunshine. The trees were leafless and brown.

I climbed on top of the rocks to view the valley below and couldn't hold back the tears. I remembered riding the Blim Birds over the waterfalls and disappearing into the rainbows, but now, the rivers and waterfalls were dry. I fell to my knees. In the distance, the Grymballian castle stood deserted.

Grymballia was dying.

Rosie bolted upright in bed and her nightshirt was drenched with sweat. She wiped her forehead and took a few deep breaths to calm down. As her heart rate slowed, her bedroom door creaked open and Maddy slipped inside.

"Can I come into your bed, Rosie?" Maddy gripped a baby doll tight to her chest.

Rosie scooted over in bed and pulled back the covers. Maddy hopped up and snuggled next to Rosie. It was the third time this week that Maddy had snuck into her room, and Rosie's third nightmare about Grymballia. Nugget licked Rosie's cheek and the three of them dozed off to a restless sleep.

The next morning, Maddy's elbow jabbed into Rosie's belly and Nugget's fuzzy ear tickled Rosie's nose. Rosie sneezed and woke everyone up. Maddy stretched and searched under the covers for Baby Zina – her newest addition to the baby world. Rosie glanced at her alarm clock.

"We better get up. Mom will be banging on the door soon for school." Rosie rubbed her eyes and hoped she did not fall asleep in history class again.

Maddy didn't say a word but rolled out of bed and shuffled to her room in zombie mode.

The dream flashed through Rosie's mind. She grabbed the acorn pendant necklace that hung around her neck. Her dreams grew worse, and her gut swirled more each day with a sense of urgency. Rosie tried to shake it off and get ready for school. She threw her long brown hair into a ponytail and wore her Living Lands and Water hoodie she earned helping to clean the Mississippi River last summer. She could already hear Lucy telling her she looked like a slob, but skirts and bows were not Rosie's style.

Downstairs, Mom flipped pancakes on the stove.

"Good morning." Her mom's voice was way too chipper for 7 a.m. as she waved her spatula at Rosie.

Rosie grunted and plopped into a chair.

"You look terrible." Her mom ignored the steaming pancakes and hurried toward Rosie. She put her hand on Rosie's forehead. "You don't feel warm. What's wrong?"

Rosie mumbled, "I'm fine, Mom. Just tired."

"Maybe you need to go to bed earlier." She looked down her nose, but then the pancakes were burning so she rushed back to the stove.

"I'm not sleeping well. I keep having nightmares."

Her mom started making a new batch of pancakes but flashed a worried look to Rosie. "Nightmares about what? School?" She tried to flip pancakes and focus on Rosie at the same time, but failed as a pancake flipped into the sink. "Whoops! I used to get a recurring nightmare that I forgot to read my book for English class. It happened every time I knew I had work to do."

Rosie knew she couldn't tell her mom what her nightmares were about. It had been six months since Grymballia, and nobody had leaked any information about their adventures. Rosie was impressed with their secret-keeping-abilities and thought they could be hired as super spies anytime soon. Her mom stared at her waiting for an answer. "Yeah, that's it. Nightmares about school."

Pancakes were placed in a perfectly stacked pile in front of Rosie. Her mom kissed her forehead. "You're a straight-A student, Rosie. Don't worry so much about school." Her mom didn't sit down to join Rosie for pancakes, but hurried back to the kitchen to clean up the mess. Her obsession with a tidy kitchen occasionally got in the way of actual eating.

Maddy hopped down the stairs, no longer a zombie, and now dressed in a pink dress and silver glittered shoes ready for second grade. Rosie would rather jump into a pile of spiders before wearing such an outfit.

"Good morning, Maddy." Her mom set a plate in front of Maddy and poured her syrup. She cut Maddy's pancake into little bites.

Rosie shook her head. Her mom treated Maddy like she was two years old cutting up her food, picking out her clothes, and cleaning her room. Maddy leaned back and enjoyed every minute.

"I'm so glad it's Friday." Rosie shoveled in her pancake and then poured on more syrup until her pancakes practically floated. "Do you think we could hike this weekend, Mom?"

Maddy sat straight up and looked to Rosie with bulging eyes. "Really! I want to go, too."

Rosie flashed Maddy a warning glance to prevent her from babbling too much information about the forest and their secret world.

Her mom finally pulled up a chair at the table and grabbed a pancake. "We can see what your dad says. He's been working extra hours, so he's gone by the time I get up each morning."

Rosie wanted to hike back to the clearing to see if anything looked different. The nightmares kept running through her head, and with every image Grymballia looked dark and deserted. "But he doesn't care if we hike alone. We used to do it all the time."

"You haven't hiked for months. Why the sudden change?" Her mom tilted her head and squinted her eyes at Rosie.

She had to think fast. "It was too hot over the summer, but now the fall air is cooler. I want to see the wildflowers and skip rocks at the creek."

Maddy bounced in her chair. "Me too! Me too! And I want to go in the cave."

Rosie coughed, choked, and a blob of pancake landed back on her plate. Gross. She glared at Maddy with eyes that could shoot fire.

Her mom didn't miss a thing. "Cave? What cave?"

Rosie avoided her mom's eyes. "Oh, um, Maddy means that she wants to crawl on the piles of rocks. Right, Maddy?" She nodded her head to Maddy, and she nodded in return. "We sometimes pretend the spaces between the big boulders are miniature caves for her dolls to live inside."

"Oh, what a cute idea." Her mom grinned and then patted Baby Zina on the head. "Maybe I'll come hiking too and see your little nature-made doll caves."

"NO!" Rosie and Maddy yelled at the same time.

Rosie continued, "We mean – it's more fun to play by ourselves."

Her mom stared at her plate and poked her pancake with her fork. "Oh, okay."

Rosie didn't want to hurt her mom's feelings, but they couldn't check on Grymballia with her there. Rosie wasn't hungry anymore and shoveled the other half of her pancake into the garbage. "I'm going to grab my backpack. The bus will be here soon."

Rosie escaped to her room and pulled out her journal. She flipped through her maps and drawings of Grymballia. The pictures of little green Giblet, Priscilla the diva spider, and the Glaperia – Xena, Dina, Trina, Gina, and Patsy made her miss her magical friends. She threw her journal into her backpack and headed downstairs to the bus.

Her stomach churned and she wasn't sure if it was the pancakes – or the nightmares.

Chapter 2

Lucy sprinted up to Rosie as soon as she stepped into the Jr. High. They had only been in eighth grade for two months and drama filled the hallways.

"Rosie, you always miss the fun around here. Tell your bus driver to skip a few stops so you can get here faster in the morning." Lucy stopped and looked Rosie up and down from head to toe. "You look like you live in a cardboard box. Would it hurt you to wear a dress every now and then?"

"I don't even own a dress," Rosie said and laughed at Lucy's shocked look.

Lucy wore a plaid pleated skirt and a white button down top. She wore black Army boots and her blonde hair was perfectly sculpted with a small plaid hat. Rosie couldn't resist getting back at her. "You look like you should be playing bagpipes."

Lucy nodded. "That's exactly the look I was going for."

They linked arms and walked toward Rosie's locker. "So what did I miss already this morning?"

Lucy's eyes grew big and she looked down the hallway to see who might be listening. "Well . . . Miranda Bytes is on a rampage."

Miranda had been in their class since the third grade. Her name was actually Miranda Bythe, but Lucy insisted on calling her "Bites" because of

Miranda's sharp personality. Miranda was intelligent and controlling, and her main focus in life was to bully Rosie. Miranda was used to winning, but Rosie beat her at the Science Fair during summer camp and Miranda was on fire.

Rosie tried not to let Miranda get to her, but she always had to watch over her shoulder and be on alert. "What do you mean that she's on a rampage? She's ALWAYS on a rampage. Did she steal Kylie's bra in gym class again or put gum in Tom's hair?"

Lucy leaned in closer. "Worse."

Rosie stared at Lucy and a bad feeling surfaced. "What did she do?"

"Miranda bought Nathan some ridiculous book about building robots." Lucy rolled her eyes. "But Nathan LOVED it."

Rosie was not surprised that Nathan would love Miranda's book because he was a builder, thinker, and he was always trying new things. "I see."

Lucy squeezed Rosie's arm. "But then she asked him to be her partner for the Science Fair this year!"

Rosie felt as if she'd been punched in the gut. "What?" She barely choked out. "What did Nathan say?"

"He didn't answer her, but he can't go with her! You and Nathan won at the Fair this summer and have to bring home the trophy again for the school year."

Rosie closed her locker and walked toward History class. Other students blurred in her vision because her brain was swimming in anger, sadness, and fear. Nathan and Rosie had built a water purification system for the Science Fair during Science Adventure week over the summer. Their system could be used for campers and travelers. Rosie developed the plan and Nathan built a small device to purify river water to drink. They won – as a team.

Lucy caught up with her and yapped in her ear. "Aren't you going to say anything? Miranda is *evil*. And you should see the ridiculous orange Converse shoes she's wearing today. They don't even match her outfit."

Rosie paused and turned to Lucy. "I don't own Nathan. If he'd rather go to the Science Fair with Miranda, then he should."

"But you two are the dynamic duo! Don't you want to be his partner again?"

Rosie blinked ten times to hold back her tears. "Of course I do!" Deep down, Rosie knew that Miranda was smart. If she got Nathan to be on her team, they would surely win the school Science Fair. Rosie and Miranda were the top two students in the class and always competing.

Rosie and Lucy filed into History class and sat toward the back of the room. Their teacher, Mr. Hack, taught in a unique way that didn't necessarily foster much learning. He sat at the front of the room and read a chapter out of the History textbook while he picked his teeth with a toothpick. He didn't believe in using their computers to assign homework or write essays, because he preferred paper. Rosie hated that so many trees could be

11

saved if Hack actually entered the modern age of teaching.

"Class, today we're going to learn about the Battle at Bunker Hill." Mr. Hack sat at his desk and began droning on as he read about the Revolutionary War.

Everyone's eyes glazed over and they leaned back in their seats to get comfortable. Some students put their heads down on their desks for their daily nap while others grabbed their cell phones and watched You Tube videos. Rosie tried to listen sometimes, but the rebellious part of her brain knew she didn't have to. The day prior to a test, Mr. Hack would give the class all of the test answers and Rosie only had to memorize them for twenty-four hours.

Rosie had a good memory but knew little history. She typically doodled in her journal or read her library book.

Lucy tapped her foot to get Rosie's attention. It was their secret way to communicate without being obvious. Rosie saw Lucy drop a tiny folded note to the floor and then cover it with her foot.

Rosie shook her head NO to Lucy. If Mr. Hack found their note he would post it on the bulletin board in the hallway. That is how the entire school found out that Isaac had a crush on Bella.

Isaac hadn't passed a note since.

Lucy ignored Rosie's protest and pushed her boot into the aisle toward Rosie. Rosie reached out with her shoe and covered the note while she slid it back toward her desk.

Transaction complete.

Rosie watched Mr. Hack's every move as she reached to the floor and grabbed the note. She opened it behind her textbook.

Rosie –
Forget about Miranda – she's nothing but a bossy bully. I'm sure you can get Nathan to be your partner for the school Science thing. Or I can be your partner and we can build special earphones that make Hack sound more interesting – an impossible experiment! LOL
Lucy

Rosie grinned. Lucy had a knack for cheering her up no matter what the situation. Rosie glanced up at Hack to see if he was watching. He continued to ramble on as he rested his head on his hand appearing bored with his own droning voice. Rosie's heart flipped with fear as she tore off a piece of paper to send a return note to Lucy.

Lucy,
I think Hack is boring himself to sleep. ☺
I don't care about Miranda.
She has beady spider eyes. Priscilla, the spider, is prettier than Miranda.
Crazy thing . . . I had another dream last night.
Rosie

Rosie wanted to talk to Lucy about the nightmares. Lucy knew about Grymballia and would understand how freaky the visions were in the dreams. Rosie folded her note, scanned the room to look for anyone watching . . .

. . . and froze. Miranda was staring from across the room and watching every move that Rosie and Lucy made. Miranda turned in her seat and leaned against the far wall to face them as she squinted with her beady, black spider eyes. Miranda knew they were passing notes. Could she feel that the notes were about her? Rosie had a flash of guilt.

Lucy tapped her foot and waved her hand for Rosie to slide over her note. Mr. Hack was yawning and paying no attention. Rosie dropped the note, covered it with her shoe, and launched it across the aisle. Lucy grabbed it as Miranda glared the entire time.

Rosie waited patiently for Lucy to read her note. She turned to Rosie and pointed to her eyes with a laugh, but then she flashed a worried look to Rosie. The nightmare.

Rosie nodded.

Mr. Hack rose from his seat and walked the room as he read from the textbook. Maisie was sound asleep on her desk and drooling on her arm while Caden was deep into a game of Fortnite on his phone. Mr. Hack didn't notice.

Rosie shook her head vigorously to Lucy to indicate they couldn't pass any notes while Hack was on the move. The rest of the class time dragged on, and Rosie was forced to learn a little about the Revolutionary War.

The bell rang and Lucy grabbed Rosie's arm and pulled her out of the classroom and into the girl's bathroom. She looked under the stalls to check for feet, and when they knew they were alone, Lucy went nuts.

"Another nightmare about Grymballia, Rosie? That's three now! It has to mean something. When Plyrim attacked, they contacted you for help. Maybe they're in trouble again. What do we do?" Lucy paced back and forth.

Rosie clenched her acorn necklace in her fist. Princess Nilly had gifted the pendant when they left Grymballia six months ago. She told Rosie that they could return to Grymballia if she rubbed the pendant, but Rosie had never used it for fear that others might discover Grymballia. She wanted to keep their magical world safe. "I don't know what it means, but each time the nightmares get worse. In this dream, everything in Grymballia looked – dead." Rosie swallowed hard. She pulled out her journal and showed Lucy. "I wrote down everything I remembered when I woke up this morning."

Lucy scanned the journal and paced again. "We need to talk to Nathan. Maybe we need to go back to Grymballia and check it out?" Lucy faced the bathroom mirror and applied more lip-gloss as she fluffed her hair. Things were never too hectic for Lucy to beautify.

"I think you're right. Maybe we should hike to the clearing and check out the cave this weekend." Rosie's insides swirled like she was on a merry-go-round. Lucy's fear intensified her own worries. What if Grymballia was in trouble? "We better get to Algebra."

Lucy groaned. "Do we have to? Algebra might as well be learning German. I'll never understand it."

Rosie tugged on Lucy's arm. "Come on." Rosie would never admit to Lucy that Algebra was one of her favorite classes – after Science of course.

As they were about to leave the bathroom, Rosie heard a scraping noise from inside a bathroom stall. "Did you hear that?" She panicked thinking of their conversation about Grymballia and if someone could have overheard.

"I didn't hear anything," Lucy said.

Rosie squatted down and looked for feet under the stalls. None. "I guess it's nothing."

Rosie and Lucy headed out the door. They didn't see the pair of orange Converse shoes appear in the middle stall as the spy stepped down off of the toilet.

Chapter 3

Rosie avoided Nathan the rest of the school day because she didn't want to know if he chose Miranda to be his Science Fair partner. She needed to talk to him about the dreams. She wondered if Nathan thought they should hike back to the clearing, or if she was overreacting. They were just dreams . . . right?

At supper that night, Maddy acted strange. Or stranger than the usual doll carrying, green monster loving, candy hoarder. She didn't eat her Jell-O with marshmallows (her favorite) and didn't bring a baby to the dinner table (unheard of in the world of Maddy.) She had dark rings under her eyes and she almost fell asleep in her mashed potatoes. It hit Rosie like a lightning bolt – Maddy was having nightmares, too.

After eating, she followed Maddy up to her room and closed the door behind her.

"Maddy, are you okay? You look tired." Rosie sat in Maddy's beanbag.

Maddy dropped her head and rubbed her eyes. She walked to her window and stared out toward their backyard forest. Silent.

"Maddy?"

She turned to Rosie with tears in her eyes. "I'm worried about Giblet."

Not what she expected. "Giblet? Why? He's safe in Grymballia."

Maddy wiped her tears. "I'm having bad dreams about Giblet."

Rosie shot to her feet. "What?" Rosie's dreams were filled with a desolate and dark Grymballia, but she never saw any of their friends in her dreams. Knowing that Maddy dreamed about Giblet made it seem more real. She knelt down in front of Maddy. "I'm having bad dreams too. What happens in your dreams, Maddy?"

Maddy grabbed a Dum-Dum sucker out of her secret stash in her underwear drawer. Dum-Dum's were her favorite, and they were also the favorite of her buddy, Giblet, the Fimbalian gatekeeper of Grymballia. After a few jolts of sugary sweetness, Maddy calmed down and slumped into her fuzzy purple chair. "I think something bad is going to happen to Giblet."

Rosie gasped. "Why would you say that?"

"In my dreams, he's not in Grymballia anymore, and my tummy feels funny every time I wake up."

"Is that why you come into my room and sleep?" Rosie kicked herself that she didn't figure it out sooner.

Maddy dropped her head. "Yeah. I get scared."

Rosie grabbed Baby Annabelle and paced the room. She needed to squeeze something while she thought about what it all meant. Deep in thought, she walked the same path back and forth multiple times and didn't realize she was tugging on Baby Annabelle's hair.

"Don't hurt her, Rosie!" Maddy grabbed her baby and wrapped her in a blanket.

"Sorry," Rosie said. Her mind was distracted thinking about what it all meant. She had dreamed that Grymballia was dark and dead, and Maddy could no longer see her best Grymballian friend. Rosie grabbed her acorn necklace.

Her fingers burned. "Ouch!" Rosie screamed and shook out her hand. The acorn pendant was hot and glowing.

"Rosie! Your necklace is lighting up!" Maddy ran toward Rosie pointing at the necklace.

Rosie ran to a mirror. The necklace was not burning her chest, but it glowed like fire. She had worn the acorn necklace from Princess Nilly ever since they left Grymballia six months ago, and it had never glowed. She grabbed it and was about to take it off, when it stopped glowing.

"What the heck was that?" Rosie didn't know if she should throw the necklace across the room or jump for joy that it was a message from Grymballia. "Something's going on, Maddy."

Maddy threw her arms around Rosie's waist and buried her head in Rosie's belly. "I'm scared, Rosie."

Rosie hugged Maddy, but couldn't admit that she was scared, too. Neither of them slept well that night.

..........*I crawled out of the cave and it was dark and gloomy. The gray sky was full of clouds and thunder rumbled. Wilted flowers and brown ferns lined the trails. Silence filled the air without tumbling waterfalls or singing birds. I walked down a path and ducked under a tree to rest against its trunk. I recognized the familiar knots and canopy.*

"Franklin?" I rubbed my hands over the tree's peeling bark. "Franklin, is this you?"

The tree rumbled and creaked and he opened his eyes only a slit. His voice was weak and tired, and I could barely hear his words.

"Help us."

Rosie bolted upright in bed, sweating, and with tears rolling down her cheeks. Fear swallowed her up and she wanted to sprint immediately through the forest, dive into the portal, and find Franklin.

"Rosie?" Maddy stood in Rosie's doorway hugging her baby.

Rosie pulled back her covers and fluffed a pillow for Maddy, and then said, "I had a bad dream again."

Maddy hurried under the covers and snuggled close. "Me, too."

Rosie scribbled the details of her dream into her journal. She knew more than ever that Grymballia was in danger and they needed to return.

The mornings got harder each day after a night of bad dreams. Rosie's mom knocked on her door to wake her up.

"Rosie, you're going to be late for the bus." Her mom flipped on her light. "Maddy? Why are you in here?"

Maddy sat up with blonde curls jutting in every direction and rubbed her eyes. "Hi, Mommy."

Rosie's body didn't want to function yet but she forced herself to sit on the edge of the bed. "Sorry, Mom. I guess I didn't hear my alarm. Maddy had a bad dream."

Her mom came and sat on the bed next to Maddy and stroked her hair. "Poor baby. What did you dream about?"

Rosie leaped up off the bed. "We better get ready mom or we'll be late for the bus. Can you make me some toast, please?" She tried to lead her mom toward the door so Maddy wasn't tempted to talk about her dream. Her mom couldn't handle dreams about missing green monsters from Grymballia at 7am.

Her mom didn't budge and waved off Rosie with annoyance. "Go and get ready, Rosie. I want to talk to Maddy a minute." She pulled Maddy into a hug. "Were you dreaming about school? What scared you?"

Maddy pulled away from her mom and got out of bed. "I'm okay, Mommy. I had a dream about . . . um . . . monsters."

"Monsters?"

Maddy glanced at Rosie. "A monster was going to do something bad to my friend."

Her mom hugged her again. "It was only a dream, Maddy."

Rosie hoped they were only dreams, but the burning pit in her gut told her otherwise.

As soon as Rosie got to school, she searched the hallways for Lucy and Nathan. There was no more time to waste; they needed to plan their return to Grymballia.

Nathan stood at his locker. Rosie tried to forget about Miranda and if Nathan might be partnering with her for a science project. She had to concentrate on Grymballia.

"Hey, Nathan." She couldn't stop her toast from twisting in her stomach.

"Hi, Rosie," he said. "What's up?"

Rosie looked up and down the hallway to assure that nobody was watching. "We need to talk." By the look on Nathan's face, Rosie knew he understood.

Lucy marched up moments later. "Hey, guys. Are you having secret meetings without me?" Lucy laughed, but the minute she saw the serious look on Rosie's face, she knew. "It happened again, didn't it?"

Nathan glanced back and forth from Lucy to Rosie. "What happened? What's going on?"

"Come on." Rosie pulled on Lucy's arm and Nathan followed close behind. After another glance down the hallway, she pulled them both into the janitor's closet and pulled the door shut.

Nathan's eye grew wide and Lucy started rambling. "What the heck, Rosie?"

Rosie opened her journal and filled in Nathan on the increasing severity of her nightmares and told them about her acorn glowing the night before. She explained that Maddy dreamed about Giblet being in danger and Franklin's plea for help.

Nathan's face dropped and he pushed up his glasses. "Why haven't you told me any of this?"

"I thought they were just dreams, but now I'm not so sure. We need to go back to Grymballia," Rosie said.

"Yes!" Nathan agreed. "But how?"

Rosie grabbed the acorn necklace. "Princess Nilly said this necklace would signal Giblet to come get us at the portal. We need to hike to the clearing tomorrow and find out what's happening."

Nathan and Lucy agreed. They would spend all weekend if necessary to assure that their friends were safe. They filed out of the janitor's closet and froze.

Miranda stood on the opposite side of the hallway leaning her back against the lockers as she drummed her fingernails against the textbook she held against her chest. One corner of her mouth rose in a sinister smirk. "Secret meetings?"

Lucy barked back. "What's it to you?"

Miranda didn't flinch. "Oh, I like secrets." She looked right into Rosie's eyes before she sauntered down the hallway.

Nathan turned to Rosie looking even more confused. "What was that all about?"

Lucy couldn't hold back her grunt. "Duh, Nathan. They're fighting over you and who will be your science partner."

Nathan's cheeks turned fifteen shades of red and he turned to Rosie. "Really? But I thought you were my partner, Rosie."

It was Rosie's turn for her face to get hot and to shift on her feet. "Yes! I would love to be your partner."

Lucy slugged Nathan's arm. "You mean you already told Miranda NO?"

"Well – of course," he said.

Rosie swelled with exhilaration and excitement. Nathan wanted to be her partner.

Lucy looked down the hallway as Miranda's orange Converse shoes strutted away. "No wonder Miranda's more evil than usual." She turned to Rosie. "We need to watch our backs. Miranda's up to something."

All three watched Miranda disappear in the crowd. Rosie quickly threw her backpack and stuff in her locker and grabbed her English folder. "We can't worry about her right now because Grymballia is more important. Let's get to class."

English class flew by and Rosie had a hard time paying attention. She found herself staring out the window and remembering her friends in Grymballia. The thought of seeing Priscilla's eight glittery shoes as she shot a web or Giblet's chubby belly and toothless smile filled her with excitement – followed soon by worry. They had better be okay.

At the end of the school day, Nathan and Lucy stood by Rosie's locker and they made plans to hike the forest trail early in the morning. Rosie grabbed her backpack and checked that she had all of her books, and then gasped. She fell to her knees and dumped everything out of her locker with books sprawling onto the floor.

"What's wrong, Rosie!" Lucy said.

"It's gone! I can't find it anywhere." Rosie frantically dug into her backpack again, and her locker sat empty with everything on the floor.

"What are you looking for?" Nathan squatted down next to Rosie.

Rosie sat with her back against the locker and her head in her hands. She breathed fast and felt dizzy. Her eyes filled with tears as she looked to her friends. "My journal. It's gone."

Shock filled Nathan and Lucy's faces and everyone realized the impact of the missing journal. It held every secret of Grymballia with drawings, details, and Rosie's recent dreams.

Grymballia could be discovered.

Chapter 4

When Rosie got home from school, she went straight to her room and passed up her mom's fresh chocolate chip cookies warm out of the oven. Her mom knew something was wrong and soon knocked on her bedroom door.

"Is everything okay, Rosie?" She sat on the edge of Rosie's bed where she curled up in a ball hugging her pillow to her chest. "Are you sick?"

The presence of her mom always made her tears fall harder. "I lost my journal. It has everything in it, Mom. I can't find it anywhere."

"Oh, honey." She pulled Rosie into a hug and Rosie sobbed. "It will turn up. I'm sure someone will find it and turn it into the office at school."

Rosie knew that wasn't true. She always put her journal in the same side pocket of her backpack. For it to be missing, someone would have to unzip her backpack and pull it out. She was positive that it couldn't fall out on its own.

Her mom looked into her eyes. "I know your journal is important to you. Maybe we can buy you a new one and start new memories?"

Rosie couldn't tell her mom the importance of her journal and its secret content about Grymballia. But she nodded. Her mom left her room to grab Rosie a warm chocolate chip cookie and to deliver it bedside.

Rosie walked to her window and looked toward the forest. She filled with guilt. What if her journal put her magical friends at risk of discovery? When her mom returned with her cookie, she immediately snapped out of her sorrow and knew she needed to take action. "Mom, Lucy and Nathan are coming over tomorrow to hike. Is that okay?"

Rosie hoped that since her mom knew she was upset about her journal, she would give permission to hike more readily.

"Sure, honey. That sounds like fun."

The rest of the evening Rosie traced all of her steps she had taken that day at school and racked her brain for any possibility that she had dropped or misplaced her journal. But every scenario placed her back at her locker before English class zipping it into her backpack. She didn't lose it, and one thing kept resurfacing in her mind . . .

Miranda.

If Miranda wanted revenge for Rosie besting her in classes and for Rosie getting Nathan as her Science partner, then Miranda knew that Rosie's journal was most important in her world. And Miranda's sneer of "Oh, I like a good secret" echoed in her mind over and over and over again.

She barely slept that night as she flipped and flopped in her bed. She couldn't wait to hike in the morning and check on her Grymballian friends. She drifted off to sleep.

.... *Help us! Help us! Screams came from far inside the forest. I recognized the voices of Tiki, Patsy - the Glaperia, and Sammy - the Larmox. The sky grew dark and thunder rumbled overhead as I walked down the forest trail. The forest mushrooms slumped and had lost their color appearing as brown lumps tucked under wilted ferns.*

I stood where the beautiful waterfall once cascaded over the rocks into a crystal clear lake below. Now, the lake was gone and there was only a puddle in the bottom of a muddy hole and a trickle of water ran over the rocks where the waterfall had once tumbled. A Blim Bird appeared from behind a tree and was barely recognizable. The Blim's colors had faded, he was losing feathers, and he was thin and wasted.

"Help us, Rosie," The Blim Bird said with a weak voice.

"What's happened here?" I asked the Blim.

The Blim Bird fell to his knees.
"Grymballia's magic was discovered."

Rosie shot up in her bed. Maddy appeared at her door. They curled up together and Rosie could feel Maddy trembling. Rosie whispered, "Tomorrow we're going back to Grymballia. We need to see if they're safe."

Maddy squeezed Rosie's hand under the covers.

The next morning, Rosie and Maddy had no problems getting out of bed knowing that they were hiking to the clearing and checking on their friends. Rosie hoped the dreams were nothing more than an overactive imagination, but she feared they signaled danger.

Nathan and Lucy arrived early and carried backpacks ready to hike. Her mom packed them lunch and wished them a good hike. If her mom only knew how important their hike was and what it all meant.

It was sunny and warmer than usual for fall and perfect for a hike. Nugget sprinted to the trail excited to return to the forest. Maddy filled her pockets with Dum-Dums hoping to see Giblet and share their favorite treat. As they stood at the trail entrance, Rosie paused.

She couldn't face Nathan and Lucy. "I had another dream last night."

They stared at Rosie and couldn't hide the fear in their eyes.

"The Blim Birds were dying and the waterfall had dried up." Rosie swallowed hard. The vivid images of her dream came rushing back to her. "The Blim Birds said that Grymballian magic had been discovered."

Nathan pushed up his glasses. "Oh, my gosh, Rosie. That's horrible."

"What if something happened to Grymballia?" Lucy said.

Rosie's stomach filled with a sense of heavy dread, but she shook her head. "No, nothing happened. They're going to be okay." She couldn't think otherwise or she might crumple on the falling leaves. "Let's go."

They hiked in silence and at a quick pace. Rosie reached for her backpack repeatedly to write in her journal about a flower or a plant, but her journal was still not there. She had packed a small notebook to record anything important, but it was not the same.

The forest was quiet. Too quiet.

Rosie stopped and looked overhead to the treetops. "Where are the birds?"

Nathan, Lucy, and Maddy paused and peered around. Silence.

Without hesitation, they hiked faster toward the clearing. Rosie took off her sweatshirt as she worked up a sweat at their fast pace. She quickly swung around to look behind them on the trail. "Did you hear that?"

Nugget barked and stood with hair straight up on the back of her neck. She stood at attention staring down the trail they had just come from.

Rosie leaned over and pet Nugget on the head. "Did you hear it too, Nugget?"

Nathan stopped and looked down the trail. "I didn't hear anything. What did you hear?"

Rosie scanned the trees and the trail but everything was still and silent. "I guess it was nothing. I thought I heard twigs snap. Maybe it was a rabbit or we scared off a deer." She turned back to continue their hike, but Lucy remained looking down the trail.

"Are you sure?" Lucy said squinting her eyes and scanning the trees.

Rosie's gut swam with uncertainty, but they couldn't waste time worrying about an animal. "I'm sure. Let's go."

When they reached the clearing, the sun reflected off of the rippling creek and a butterfly sat on a cluster of flowers. Rosie hoped it was a good sign. She grasped her acorn pendant. It had been quiet and cold ever since it glowed the other night.

Maddy immediately headed toward the cave without waiting for the rest of them. Everyone followed.

Inside the cave, nothing had changed. They flipped on their flashlights and damp rocks surrounded the darkness without signs of life.

"Now what do we do?" Lucy said. "We need Giblet to come open the portal."

Rosie rubbed the acorn. "Princess Nilly told us that the acorn would call Giblet to come get us." She squeezed the acorn pendant and looked down to her chest where it rested. "Giblet? Princess Nilly? Are you out there?" She felt silly talking to her chest.

They stood waiting, but nothing happened.

Maddy pounded on the cave walls and screamed, "Giblet! Where are you?"

"Shhhh!" Nathan said. "I hear something."

Music flowed from beyond the cave. Rosie filled with relief to recognize the peaceful songs of Grymballia. "I hear it!" She pulled out her notebook as the tune flowed.

Our friends of Grymballia, we are safe,
But evil from your world looms.
If Grymballian magic is discovered,
Our beautiful land is doomed.
We request your presence to face the threat,
We need to make a plan.
The acorn's light is your calling card,
Through the portal to our land.

The song ended and silence filled the cave. Rosie scratched down every last word on her notepad, and they huddled together to read it again. Overwhelming relief filled Rosie as she repeated the first line, "Our friends of Grymballia, we are safe." They were okay.

Nathan said, "Somehow we need to use the acorn to get inside. You already rubbed it and talked to it, what else can we do?"

Lucy laughed nervously, "Do you need to kiss the acorn or dance around with it?"

Rosie grasped the acorn pendant and unhooked the clasp of the necklace. She cupped the chain and pendant in her palm and kissed the acorn.

"I was kidding! I can't believe you just kissed the acorn." Lucy bent over laughing.

Rosie didn't crack a smile. "I'll do whatever it takes." She hoped her journal wasn't the reason Grymballia was in danger.

Maddy whined, "Where's Giblet? Can't he come get us?"

Rosie squeezed the acorn necklace tight and closed her eyes. She envisioned the Glaperia, Spike and his brothers Rufus and Dennis, and the snakes - Kimmie and Lila. Her heart filled with warmth at the memory of her friends and she whispered, "Grymballia, we want to return to your world. She recited the song that Giblet used to enter Grymballia in the past:

Land of the Earth, we have come forth,
We bear no harm and promise our worth.

Nature's our friend; we will never neglect
Grymballia we enter and always protect.

Light filled the cave and Rosie's acorn glowed bright. The corner of the cave became a churning ball of brightness as the portal formed. Before they knew what was happening, Giblet jumped out of the portal and into the cave.

"Giblet!" Maddy pounced on top of him and tackled him into the dirt with a hug.

Nugget barked in a frenzy of excitement.

Giblet's toothless grin spread across his smooth green face as he waved flattened underneath Maddy. "Hello, friends. We're happy you called. We've been waiting for your contact."

Rosie furrowed her brow. "You've been waiting for us to call?"

Maddy relaxed and then stood back up while holding onto Giblet's hand. Giblet jumped to his feet and pointed toward the portal. "Princess Nilly needs to see you right away. Shall we return to Grymballia?"

Rosie filled with excitement. She had been waiting to return to Grymballia for months, and now was her chance.

Nobody hesitated. Lucy and Nathan dove through the portal and Maddy leaped in by herself. Rosie grabbed Nugget and climbed into the glowing tunnel. The whirling wind and suction pulled her quickly off of her feet as she was carried toward Grymballia. She landed with a thump in the dirt on the other side. Giblet soon followed.

They brushed the dirt off of their clothes and practically ran to the cave entrance to see Grymballia again. As Rosie turned the corner of the cave, her nightmares of a barren and desolate Grymballia rushed through her mind . . .

. . .but Grymballia was beautiful. Rosie wanted to dance and sing because the sun glowed bright in a sky filled with rainbows. The waterfall's turbulent flow crashed into the large lake in the valley below, and the golden castle gleamed in the distance.

"I'm so happy that Grymballia is okay!" Rosie threw her arms in the air.

Princess Nilly flitted out of the trees and greeted them with smiles. "Friends, we are so happy you have returned."

Maddy followed Giblet wherever he walked and Rosie saw her slide him a Dum-Dum sucker secretly so that the princess couldn't see.

"Princess Nilly, we've missed you so much," Rosie said.

The princess flew straight to Rosie with a grave look on her face. "Rosie, what do you mean that you're happy that Grymballia is okay?" Princess Nilly glanced to Giblet with a flutter and nervous look that Rosie had never seen on the princess before.

Rosie turned to Maddy. She dropped her head as Maddy squeezed Giblet's hand.

"Princess Nilly, Maddy and I have had some nightmares about Grymballia."

Princess Nilly zipped back and forth faster than ever and her voice was high pitched and strained. "Oh, no. Oh, no! We must make our way to the castle. Come, immediately."

Rosie was scared. She hadn't even told Princess Nilly what her dreams were about, and she could see that Grymballia was fine! She nervously reached for her acorn necklace.

It was gone.

"My acorn pendant is gone! It must have fallen out of my hand when I went through the portal." Rosie sprinted back into the cave and crawled around on the dirt floor. She couldn't find it anywhere.

Lucy squatted down next to her and looked around. "Did you find it?"

Rosie stood up. "No. I had it in my hand when we called for Giblet, and now its gone."

Princess Nilly flew into the cave. "We must get to the castle. Please, come."

Rosie looked to Lucy with surprise. Princess Nilly had never been so pushy before. She whispered to Lucy, "What's going on?"

Lucy replied, "I don't know, but the princess needs to chill out."

Princess Nilly sang into the air and Blim Birds appeared on the horizon. They landed in front of their group for a quick flight to the castle.

The Blim Birds' wings jutted out from their cat-like body. They were multi-colored like the rainbows where they often hid. Maddy and Giblet hopped onto a Blim Bird and Rosie saw them sneaking a Dum-Dum sucker for the ride. Orange drool dribbled down Giblet's chin as their Blim Bird took off.

Rosie hated to leave without her necklace, but had no choice. She soared through the air as she scratched the soft, colorful fur on her Blim Bird. Grymballia drifted by below filled with colors, trees, villages, and full of life. The dead world of her nightmares was nowhere in sight – so why was Princess Nilly in such a hurry?

They landed in front of the castle and a surprise awaited them. All of their friends cheered as the Blim Birds landed. Nugget ran straight toward her friend, Sid, who had an innocent pink and fluffy coat but a mouth full of razor-sharp teeth. They bound around in circles and chased each other's tail.

"Hello, darlings." Priscilla, the spider, waved four of her red glittered boots as she flipped a boa around her neck. She shot a web to a nearby tree branch and zipped over their heads while waving her hat. Priscilla had mad skills with her web and had used her web to trip the Flagerian and wrap up Plyrim soldiers.

"Hi, Priscilla!" Rosie waved as the diva spider sat on her web.

Tiki, the water turk, waved his flippered hand; while Sammy, the Larmox, waved his top hat. The other Larmox, Henry and Jojo, peeked their heads out of their burrowed holes as they had just arrived to the party. The Glaperia – Xena, Dina, Trina, Nina, and Patsy flew overhead with their many eyes shining bright in welcome. Kimmie and Lila slithered toward the gathered group, and Spike, Rufus, and Dennis rolled up next to them.

"Everyone is here!" Lucy threw up her hands and hugged everyone she greeted.

Maddy stuck to Giblet as he stood next to his twin brother, Goblet.

Rosie couldn't stop smiling and was overwhelmed to see all of her friends. It's as if she had been missing a part of herself that she was able to get back, and she now felt whole again.

Princess Nilly flew overhead. "Attention, everyone. Please come into the castle so we can discuss matters in more detail."

Rosie's heart sank. It was not a welcoming party; there was need for a gathering. Everyone filed into the castle immediately and followed her request. The golden castle beamed with its gold plates and solar panels that powered all of Grymballia. Purple, blue, and pink flowers scattered the landscape and their fragrance filled Rosie's nose as she inhaled a deep breath. Trees sculpted into knights, ladybugs, fish, and the sun stood at the castle entrance.

Inside the castle, the King and Queen sat on their thrones looking regal and respected. Hanging overhead, the sun crafted of yellow daffodils and daisies bloomed bright adding warmth to the room. The King lifted off of his throne flitting his wings and held up his twig arms. "Welcome back to Grymballia, my friends, it is so wonderful to have you back. You have a special place in our hearts, because without you there would be no Grymballia. You defeated Plyrim and rescued us from the Fligarian. That day will forever be remembered in our Grymballian history." The King spoke loudly and proudly as he addressed Rosie and her friends.

Rosie's cheeks flushed with the attention. Nathan held up his head proudly and Lucy bowed.

"Thank you very much." Rosie managed to say to the King. "We're so happy to be back."

Princess Nilly hovered next to her mother and father's thrones. Everyone in the room immediately quieted and turned toward the princess. "I need your attention. We have matters to discuss."

"What's going on, Princess Nilly? My dreams must have been wrong, because Grymballia is fine." Rosie shrugged her shoulders.

"Grymballia is in danger," Princess Nilly said. "This time the danger comes from outside our walls. When Plyrim threatened Grymballia, we came to you for help. There are only a chosen few in the world that respect nature, look at it with awe and wonder, and see its beauty with special eyes. You are one of those people, Rosie."

Rosie shifted nervously on her feet and looked to Lucy for support. Lucy shrugged her shoulders. Rosie now realized that the Grymballians had specifically sought her out to help them with Plyrim. She had assumed it was pure luck that she heard their songs from the forest when they needed help.

Princess Nilly continued, "You did not hesitate to save Grymballia. We also welcomed your friends and Maddy as part of our Grymballian family. We know that our secrets and magic are safe with you. But if someone we did not choose from the outside world were to know of Grymballia's magic, then Grymballia's magic would be lost."

A dreadful pit returned to Rosie's stomach. Her journal with Grymballia's secrets was missing – or stolen.

"Princess Nilly, what would happen if you lost your magic?" Nathan asked.

"Initially, everyone would lose their powers, and then the sun would not shine. We would lose our ability to power Grymballia without sunlight, and our beautiful land would die. We would have to find another land to live on, but the trees and flowers would perish."

Rosie remembered Franklin in her dream. He would not be able to leave Grymballia and would die in darkness.

Nathan pushed up his glasses. "Princess Nilly, how do you know your world is at risk?"

Princess Nilly motioned for them to follow her. "I will show you. Come my friends, let us show you a part of Grymballia you have not yet experienced."

Chapter 5

Seeing a secret part of Grymballia filled Rosie with excitement and anticipation. She couldn't imagine anything more beautiful than what she had already seen. Nathan and Lucy bounced anxiously on their toes as they looked to each other. The King placed his hand on a pinecone that topped his throne, and he turned it three times counterclockwise. The floral sun hanging overhead began to glow and the floor began to shake as a small door appeared in the wall behind the King's throne. The door lifted from the floor slowly and light glowed from beyond.

"Come, my friends. Please watch your head. The door is Grymballia size." The Princess smiled and flew into the small mysterious doorway.

Nugget zipped into the doorway after Princess Nilly. Rosie looked to Nathan and Lucy and they ducked into the tiny door. Maddy stayed by Giblet and the entire mass of Grymballian friends followed into the secret passageway.

Lucy said, "Where do you suppose this leads?"

"I don't know." Rosie smelled damp air and the walls inside the passageways were surrounded by stone. It was as if they were walking deeper into the earth.

Nathan said, "We're lucky they trust us with their secrets."

They climbed down a steep stairway of polished stones, and the walls glowed with lanterns lit with lightning bugs. It was warm and the air was heavy like a greenhouse. Rosie heard a loud rumbling up ahead and light glimmered at the bottom of the stairs. Kimmie, the snake, slid down the steps next to Rosie glowing bright to help light the way.

"Thanks, Kimmie," Lucy said.

At the bottom of the stairs, the rumbling sound increased and sounded like a collection of drums in the distance. Princess Nilly motioned them forward into a tunnel lined on each side by massive tree trunks projecting limbs overhead to form an arch. As Rosie walked under the leaves and vines of the natural arch, the light intensified up ahead and the sound grew louder.

They soon stepped into an immense chamber. Rosie's mouth dropped open as she looked around. They stood in a beautiful oasis underneath the castle.

Plush green grass and fresh white petunias and pink tulips lined the ground while butterflies and birds flew around. Above their heads, the tall chamber was open to the sky and warm sunlight poured inside.

Lucy tilted up her head and twirled around. "You have an underground secret garden!"

Princess Nilly grinned.

The scent of flowers filled the air and trees grew inside the castle. In the center of the room, the tumbling waterfall focused everyone's attention. Five small streams flowed from behind rocks and these joined into one massive waterfall cascading down a bluff into the blue pool of water below. The overhead sun caught the sprays of water and rainbows filled the room.

Rosie could only say, "Wow."

Princess Nilly flew around with excitement and pride. "This is Paradise Cove," she explained. "This hidden chamber is a source of magic and power. Come with me to the falls, and I'll show you."

They followed the princess.

"I've only been here once before," Tiki whispered to Rosie as he waddled alongside her. "It's such a special place. I came when my son, Pico, was gravely ill. Paradise Cove showed us what to do and directed us to the MickeyBerry Root to cure him."

"I'm so happy your son is okay, Tiki. It must be a magical place." Rosie tried to look ahead to see where Princess Nilly was leading them. How could a place be so powerful?

Patsy, the Glaperian, flew next to Rosie. "Paradise Cove helped our family, too. Xena, Dina, Trina, Gina, and I developed a sickness that blurred our vision. We could no longer see through objects, and we were getting weaker. Princess Nilly brought us to Paradise Cove. The waterfall showed us that the flowers where we lived were making us ill because they were infested with Luggar mites. We moved to different flowers and we were instantly cured."

Rosie slowly understood. The waterfalls at Paradise Cove solved problems, but could it predict the future?

Princess Nilly approached the waterfall and the falling water parted to reveal a hidden passage tucked underneath. She directed everyone to follow her under the falls.

Once safe underneath the falls, the water poured over top of their heads with great force and it was hard to hear each other. Giblet smacked his tail three times and when sparks flew, the sound of rumbling water silenced. Princess Nilly spoke.

"Welcome to Paradise Cove. The waterfall has a special power to respond to your questions with an image. It may show you something occurring in the present, but if it refers to the future, the image will be less clear. We only use the waterfall in time of urgency."

Princess Nilly walked up to the back of the waterfall and spoke:

Powerful water, we ask of you
To tell us what you see.
We respect your vision and your power
And will always protect thee.

Princess Nilly held out her hands and let the water tumble over her fingertips. Water splashed into her face, but she didn't flinch. The water began to glow. She spoke again.

"Paradise Cove and Great Waterfall, please show us the home of Rosie and Maddy." Princess Nilly looked at Rosie and smiled.

The waterfall glowed, but soon the blanket of water changed as an image appeared on the water's surface. Rosie thought it was as if she was watching a real time moving starring her own home. She recognized her kitchen, her refrigerator, her . . .

"Daddy! That's Daddy!" Maddy jumped up and down and pointed to the images on the water.

"He can't hear you, Maddy," Princess Nilly said. "This is what's happening at your house right now, but they don't know we are watching. We do not use the Great Waterfall to spy on your family, but we do check to assure that you are safe."

The picture faded away when Princess Nilly waved her hands.

Lucy approached Princess Nilly and rubbed her palms together in front of her face. "Can I ask it something? I want to know next week's Powerball numbers!"

"Lucy!" Nathan rolled his eyes.

Princess Nilly remained calm. "I'm sorry, Lucy. We don't use the Great Waterfall in that way."

Lucy crossed her arms over her chest and looked to Rosie. "Just think what we could do with this? I could become a millionaire or at least Ace my algebra test."

Rosie ignored Lucy. Deep down she knew that Lucy wouldn't abuse the waterfall in that way.

Princess Nilly rested her hand on Rosie's shoulder. "The Great Waterfall led us to you, Rosie."

She looked with shock. "What?"

"When we were attacked by Plyrim, we asked the Great Waterfall for help. It showed us your image. It chose you to save us."

Rosie felt nauseated and a little dizzy. She turned to the glowing waterfall and suddenly wondered where its power came from and how it would have chosen her. "Um, that's too weird."

Goblet stepped forward. "It made perfect sense to us. The Great Waterfall showed us what you do to protect the environment through planting trees, recycling, cleaning ditches, and composting. You act the same as we do, but live on the outside world."

Spike nudged her arm. "You're an honorary Grymballian."

Rosie swelled inside and her nerves calmed. She blushed and dropped her head. "I'm honored."

Princess Nilly placed her hands in the waterfall again as she spoke. "I need to show you why I'm worried about Grymballia." The water glowed. "Future predictions are uncertain and blurry," she said to Rosie and then turned back to the falls. "Great Waterfall, is Grymballia safe?"

The waterfall shifted and lights whirled as a blurry image of Grymballia developed. The outlines were not as clear as the image of Rosie's kitchen, but they recognized a rainbow and trees. Instantly, the image grew dark and gray and a scream echoed out from the image. Then it disappeared.

"What was that?" Nathan asked.

Princess Nilly fidgeted and flew back and forth. "We don't know. We've repeated the question many times and each time Grymballia turns dark and then disappears. I'm afraid we're in danger and that's why we were happy to see you."

Rosie's stomach plummeted to her toes. "Do you think its related to my nightmares, Princess Nilly?"

"Are your dreams similar to these images?"

Rosie didn't want to answer. The images in the waterfall of the black and desolate Grymballia matched the destruction she saw in her dreams. "Yes."

Princess Nilly flew like a lightning bolt directly to Rosie's face.

"You have seen the destruction of Grymballia in your dreams? You ARE the chosen one!"

"There's more, Princess. Maddy's been having dreams about Giblet." Rosie looked at Giblet to make sure he was prepared. "She dreamed that Giblet was taken from Grymballia." She threw her hands in the air. "But they're just dreams, Princess Nilly!"

Maddy wrapped her arms around Giblet and he looked stunned and shaken.

"I'll be okay, Miss Maddy." Giblet tugged on her pigtail gently like he was trying to remove the nightmare from her brain.

The mass of Grymballians chattered and a sense of panic spread across the room.

Princess Nilly reacted, "Giblet, you must be on high alert. You're at risk when you transport the children back and forth through the portal, so be extremely careful."

"Yes, Princess Nilly," Giblet replied.

Princess Nilly turned to Rosie. "You're our only protection from the outside world. If our magic world is discovered, Grymballia and everyone in it will be destroyed."

Rosie felt sick. "We would never let that happen."

"I know you will protect us," Kimmie said.

"That's why you're all so special to us." Sid rested a paw on Nugget.

"You must return to your world, but warn us of any threat so we can prepare."

They hiked out of the secret chamber and collected in front of the castle. Princess Nilly sang a tune and the Blim Birds arrived.

Spike spoke, "Rosie, we're not afraid to fight. We would go to battle again with you any day. If someone is coming, let us know." He shot the sharp spikes out of his smooth yellow body to demonstrate his battle gear.

"Yes, darling, I'm not afraid to soil my boots in battle." Priscilla spun a web on the statue of Mother Nature.

Rosie hopped on a Blim Bird. "We'll do our best to protect Grymballia. You are dear friends and we would never let anyone hurt you." Rosie reached up to her neck and remembered in panic. "Princess Nilly! I dropped my acorn necklace when we came through the portal. How will we get back into Grymballia?"

Princess Nilly dipped from the sky and onto a flower. Her face was filled with fear. "It's gone?"

Rosie stammered, "I – I – hope it's in the cave on our side of the portal. I just dropped it." It was a much bigger mistake than Rosie realized.

Princess Nilly could not look into Rosie's eyes. "It's the only way back. There is only one acorn pendant unless Giblet comes to get you first."

It sunk in. They had no way to return unless they found the necklace. Giblet could come get them, but they would never know when he was there.

"I will find the necklace, Princess Nilly. Don't worry." But Rosie *was* worried. Very worried.

As they flew away from the castle, their Grymballian friends waved their flippers, glittered boots, or wings. Rosie waved back with a heavy sense of responsibility to protect them all from her own world. She had to find the acorn necklace and her journal. Guilt caused her stomach to churn, if anyone discovered Grymballia due to her mistakes, she could never forgive herself.

Giblet sucked on his last Dum-Dum as they stood at the cave. Rosie loved that Princess Nilly ignored Giblet's sweet treats while they visited – she was certain the princess knew.

They hugged and patted the Blim Birds to say good-bye and headed into the cave. Inside the cave, Giblet wiped the purple sucker goo from his chin and scratched the familiar pattern on the cave floor. He drew the arch and sun with its projecting rays. He chanted:

Land of the Earth, we must leave you now,
We keep all your secrets, we solemnly vow.
Nature's our friend and we will never neglect
Grymballia we now leave and always protect.

The portal glowed bright. Maddy made no movement toward the portal and stood right next to Giblet.

"I'm staying here." Maddy grabbed Giblet's arm.

"We'll see Giblet again soon. Giblet will come get us if we need him. We have to go home now." Rosie used her soft, gentle voice instead of the big sister hurry-the-heck-up voice.

"But you lost the acorn necklace, Rosie! We can't get back in." Maddy was smarter than Rosie thought, and she didn't budge.

"We'll find it. I'm sure it's waiting on the other side sitting in the dirt." Rosie crossed her fingers and toes, hoping it were true.

Maddy turned to Giblet. "This is for you, Giblet. It's the last one." She handed him the last Root Beer flavored Dum-Dum sucker.

Nathan and Lucy slid through the portal. Rosie wanted Maddy to go first so she didn't attempt to stay in Grymballia forever. Maddy gave Giblet one last squeeze and zipped into the swirling light.

Rosie held Nugget at the portal entrance. "Good-bye, Giblet. Please be careful. It sounds like something wants to hurt you or Grymballia. We'll come to the cave if we have any news." She gave Giblet a hug and Nugget licked his cheek.

"I'll be careful, Rosie." Giblet nodded.

Rosie leaped into the light and jumped into the portal. Dizzy and upside down she fell out into the cave on the other side. Nugget bolted out of her arms, and Rosie dropped to her knees and searched the dirt.

The acorn necklace was nowhere in sight.

Chapter 6

"What's wrong, Rosie?" Nathan said.

"The acorn necklace is gone." Rosie wanted to cry. "Where could it be?"

Nathan's face told Rosie that he knew it was serious. If someone else got a hold of the necklace, then they would also have access to Grymballia. It was bad enough that her journal was missing, but now the was acorn too. Rosie sat on a boulder with her head in her hands.

Nathan scooted next to her. "It'll be okay. We'll find it." He elbowed her. "Because you're the chosen one." He laughed.

Rosie couldn't help but smile. "Isn't that hilarious? Me – the chosen one?"

"Actually, it makes perfect sense to me," Nathan said.

Nugget bolted toward the trees barking. Rosie jumped to her feet.

"Something's out there, Rosie. I heard it." Maddy ran to Rosie's side and gripped her hand.

"Nugget!" Rosie yelled. Nugget had stopped at the trail but stared into the dense trees. Rosie heard a rustle from the bushes and Nugget started barking again.

"I heard it, too!" Lucy said.

Nathan charged forward toward the trees and Rosie followed on his heels. They scanned the forest and Nugget sniffed every fern and bush, but nothing was there.

"I have a bad feeling about this," Rosie whispered to Nathan. "It can't be coincidence that something is out here when my necklace is missing."

"It could have been a squirrel or a rabbit. Don't beat yourself up," he said, but not convincingly.

The others joined them and Nugget stopped barking. Whatever made the noise was gone. They gathered their things and started the hike home. Rosie couldn't settle her brain and she continuously checked her neck for the necklace. It wasn't there.

When they reached their backyard, Nugget bounded to the back door and Maddy reunited with Baby Tilly on the swing. As Rosie walked toward the house, she scanned every inch of the grass hoping to catch a glimpse of her necklace even though she knew she had it in the cave before they went to Grymballia.

Rosie's dad walked onto the back patio. "Hey there, hikers. Do you all want to stay for burgers for supper?" He was lighting the grill and waving his spatula.

Lucy's face lit up. "Yeah! Let me call my dad and see if it's okay."

Nathan nodded. "I would love to."

Rosie's sour mood lifted. Lucy got the okay from her dad and they headed to Rosie's room to talk about the day.

Maddy opted to have a massive five-doll disco party in her room with the music blaring, so she didn't join them. Nathan plopped in Rosie's papa-san chair and grabbed her globe on his lap. He spun it and searched the world.

Lucy wandered Rosie's room and fiddled with her science trophies and pottery crafts. Rosie sat on her bed and leaned against her headboard.

"We will have to keep our eyes open for anything strange. I can't imagine anything bad happening to Grymballia." Rosie looked toward the trees out her window.

Lucy grabbed a stuffed sloth and hugged it to her chest. "But it's not like you wouldn't notice someone walking through your woods to get to the cave – right? That's how someone would have to get in."

"Right. But I can't watch it twenty-four hours a day. And what if the noises we heard was somebody out there spying on us?"

Nathan's face lit up and he tried to jump out of his chair, but the cushy papa-san chair made him look more like a seal flopping out of water. "I have an idea!"

"What?" Lucy said.

"What if we set a trap? We can rig an alarm to detect anyone moving inside the cave that might try to harm Grymballia." Nathan paced the room and Rosie could actually see the cogwheels spinning in his head.

Rosie hopped off the bed filled with excitement. "What a great idea! Can you do that?" It was a silly question. Nathan was an engineering whiz and gadgets were his specialty.

Nathan smirked. "Of course."

Lucy and her stuffed sloth chimed in. "But wouldn't every deer, rabbit, or sloth that wandered into the cave also set off the alarm?"

Nathan paused his pacing. "Probably, but I don't think many animals likely go into the cave. It's a chance we have to take."

"When? We need to get it set up as soon as possible." Rosie wanted to head out after supper and hoped her parents wouldn't forbid her to hike in the darkness. At least it was the weekend. "Can you guys come over again tomorrow?"

Nathan stopped and stared at Rosie's ceiling and didn't speak for a solid minute. Rosie glanced at Lucy and shrugged. Then, he snapped out of it. "I have to go to church, and then I can get the supplies at the hardware store and be here by eleven. Does that work?"

"Works for me," Lucy said.

"Perfect." Rosie filled with hope that things were going to be okay and they could protect Grymballia. Her dad yelled from downstairs that the burgers were hot and ready to eat.

They devoured their food and chatted over dinner as if all was well with the world – or worlds. Rosie temporarily forgot about her missing journal and the lost acorn necklace. Her dad told silly jokes that Nathan thought were hilarious, and Maddy pulled Baby Annabelle's high chair to the table and fed her mini burger bites.

"Everyone ready for dessert?" Rosie's mom carried cheesecake topped with fresh strawberries and Lucy groaned with delight.

After they shoveled in cheesecake, they leaned back in their chairs rubbing their distended bellies.

"I'm stuffed. Thank you Mr. and Mrs. Montgomery," Nathan said.

"Yes, thank you," Lucy chimed in as she groaned again but this time in misery.

"You're welcome." Rosie's mom started clearing the table. "Give me ten minutes to clear the table and I can run you kids home."

Rosie carried her plate to the dishwasher, and Nathan and Lucy followed her lead. They ran upstairs to make final plans.

Rosie grabbed her backup notepad and jotted down notes. She felt that a part of her was missing without her journal, and the recesses of her brain still traced her steps wondering where she had left it. She couldn't shake the bad feeling lingering in her gut. "Do you guys think someone stole my journal?"

Lucy didn't hesitate. "Duh, I'm sure it was Miranda."

Nathan's face appeared shocked with wide eyes and mouth dropping open. "Why would you think Miranda took it?"

"Oh, sweet Nathan, Miranda is a psychopath," Lucy said.

Nathan squirmed and shifted on his feet. "She's . . . kind of pushy at times, I guess."

Rosie and Lucy laughed simultaneously.

Nathan scrunched his eyebrows. "I don't get it?"

Rosie explained. "Miranda is not a psychopath." She flashed Lucy a look. "But she can't stand it when I beat her at any test or project. She takes it personally and swears revenge every time."

Nathan chuckled. "Really?"

Rosie threw up her arms. "It's not funny! I think she might have stolen my journal when you told her you wouldn't be her partner for the Science Fair."

"You really think she would stoop that low?"

Lucy and Rosie nodded immediately. Lucy added, "Miranda has a screw loose."

Nathan tilted his head and started wringing his hands. "If that's the case, would Miranda read your journal and expose Grymballia?"

Rosie's stomach dropped. It's what she feared and hearing Nathan say it out loud made it real. "I don't know."

Lucy turned her back to Rosie and Nathan.

"Lucy, what's wrong?" Rosie asked.

Lucy turned around slowly with a horrible look on her face. "There's something I've never told you guys." She dropped her head and stared at the carpet. "I have history with Miranda."

Rosie glanced to Nathan, but kept quiet to let Lucy continue.

"When we were in fourth grade, Miranda lived two houses down from mine. She had a pet squirrel that she raised after it fell out of a tree. His name was Ralph, and he was adorable." Lucy still couldn't look toward Rosie. She sat on the edge of the bed.

"One morning, Ralph escaped his cage in Miranda's garage and ran across the yard - just as my dad was backing out of the garage. He hit Ralph and he died." Lucy had tears falling down her cheeks. "It was so awful! Miranda came out of her house screaming at the same time I came out of my house. She blamed me for killing Ralph and has hated me ever since." Lucy buried her head in her hands.

"But you didn't kill Ralph, Lucy. Why would she blame you? It was an accident." Rosie sat next to Lucy and rubbed her back.

Nathan said, "It sounds like Miranda's been building up her anger for a long time."

They all looked to each other. Rosie knew that Miranda had her journal.

"I'm going to get to work on our motion detector to protect Grymballia." Nathan headed toward the bedroom door.

Lucy stood up, wiped her cheeks, and composed self. "We need to watch our backs, Rosie."

"I agree. We can't let Miranda or anyone else enter Grymballia – or our friends will die."

Chapter 7

Rosie had no nightmares that night because she didn't sleep. Tossing and turning she couldn't help but feel responsible for Grymballia being in danger. She hoped they were wrong about Miranda and that her journal would show up at school on Monday.

Lucy and Nathan arrived at her house late morning as planned. Nathan carried a large duffel bag filled with supplies and Lucy came with cupcakes.

"Cupcakes for a hike?" Rosie joked.

"There is never a wrong time for cupcakes." Lucy pranced in her fashion hiking boots and her hair was filled with so much gel, it didn't move as she pranced toward the house.

"Do you need help carrying all of that?" Rosie asked Nathan.

"No, I'm good." Nathan swung the duffel bag over his shoulder with a grunt.

Rosie packed a picnic lunch to eat at the clearing in the forest. Maddy met them in the kitchen dressed in overalls and ready to hike. "I want to come too, Rosie."

"Okay, Maddy." Rosie looked around to assure her mom wasn't listening. "Did you have any bad dreams last night?"

Maddy shook her head. "Nope. That means Giblet is okay, right Rosie?"

"We'll keep Giblet safe." *I hope* – Rosie thought to herself.

After her mom gave her typical speech warning them about bugs, sunscreen, swimming, and the Loch Ness Monster they headed off on the trail. It was a beautiful fall day and the sun radiated through the red and gold trees that were dropping leaves. Nugget bounded down the trail ahead of them, like usual, and sniffed at every clump of dirt and bush. Lucy stuck to the middle of the trail to avoid getting her fancy boots dirty.

"Were you able to figure out something for the cave?" Rosie asked Nathan. She knew that his engineering and mechanically inclined brain loved this mission.

"I hope so." Nathan readjusted the heavy duffel bag. "I got a trail camera that deer hunters use that uses a motion detector, and then I'm going to rig it up to an app on my cell phone called Watcher. It will send an alarm if something triggers the motion detector."

"Wow. That sounds pretty cool." Rosie was impressed. "But if the motion detector goes off in the cave and we are far away, how can we stop someone in time before they get into Grymballia?"

"That's the second part of my trap." Nathan's face lit up. "If the motion detector goes off, then a net will drop from the roof of the cave and trap whoever is there."

"That's genius. What if we trap Giblet as he comes out of the portal?" Rosie asked.

Nathan stopped on the trail. "I didn't think about that. I was trying to prevent someone getting INTO Grymballia and didn't think about someone coming out."

Lucy had been listening and chimed in. "I don't think we can worry about that. If Giblet happens to come out to our world, the motion detector will signal us and we will get him out of the net. But if someone is trying to get into Grymballia, they could all die. We have to take that chance."

"I agree." Rosie nodded.

Nathan nodded and they walked again.

Maddy stopped up ahead and stared into the trees. Rosie followed her gaze and saw a flash of red, but then it was gone.

"What are you looking at?" Lucy stood next to Rosie staring into the woods.

"I thought I saw something." Rosie said. "Did you see something, Maddy?"

Maddy squatted down next to Nugget who also stared into the trees with ears pointed straight into the air. "There's someone out there, Rosie."

Rosie filled with fear. Was someone following them? She hurried toward Maddy and looked into the trees from her view. "What did you see, Maddy?"

Maddy pointed. "Someone ran that way wearing a red jacket and black hat."

"Could you see their face? Was it a boy or a girl?" Rosie wanted to know everything.

"I don't know, Rosie. It happened too fast."

Nathan, Lucy, and Rosie scoured the area and nobody saw anyone in the trees or heard any rustling in the bushes.

Nathan said, "I don't know what or who it was, but I think we better install the alarm system soon."

They practically ran the rest of the trail to the clearing. They didn't bother skipping rocks at the creek or dipping their toes in the water. Walking straight into the cave, Nathan opened his bag and spread out its contents on the dirt floor.

"How can we help?" Rosie said.

"I need you guys to rig up the net on the roof of the cave. I will show you how to link a trigger wire to the alarm after you get it secure."

Lucy rolled her eyes. "I have no idea what all of that means, but I'll follow you Rosie."

Nathan grabbed electronic gadgets, screwdrivers, batteries, and buried his head in wires as he fashioned the motion detector. Rosie grabbed the net and surveyed the roof of the cave in the area where the portal appeared. "If we use a special drill bit, we should be able to screw a hook into the ceiling to hang the net. Then, when the alarm is triggered, it will pull the net off of the hooks to drop on whoever is standing here."

"How do you know how to do that?" Lucy said sarcastically.

"How do you know how to make that fancy marbled glitter color on your fingernails?" Rosie grinned as Lucy admired her nails. "We all have special talents."

Maddy stood at the cave opening. "I want to help, too."

The thought of the person in the red jacket lurking in the woods lingered in Rosie's mind.

"Maddy, how about you stand there and watch for anyone coming?"

"Okay." Maddy peeked around the corner of the cave entrance. "I don't see anything."

They worked fast and the cold, damp cave made Rosie's fingers cramp as she used the tools. Nathan worked quietly as he concentrated on the motion detector and fiddled with his phone. Rosie admired his genius to figure the system out.

When the net was secured overhead, Rosie sat on the cave floor just as Nathan said, "Okay, I think I've got it."

He stretched a thin wire up to the hanging net, pushed a few buttons on his phone, and then triggered a button on the motion detector. A green light appeared on the device. "Okay, let's test it out."

Nathan waved his hand in front of the motion detector. The light flashed red and his phone alarmed with a loud squeal that echoed off of the cave walls. Maddy covered her ears. The net dropped from the ceiling and fell onto Rosie's head and dropped her to the floor.

The heavy net made it impossible for Rosie to sit up. "Um, I think it works."

Lucy and Nathan removed the net and helped Rosie off of the floor.

"That was so awesome!" Lucy helped Nathan rig the net up to the ceiling.

Rosie brushed off the dirt. "It worked great, Nathan. Good job."

Nathan reset the alarm and they stepped out of the cave. Maddy bounced around and laughed. "Rosie, you got caught! Can I try?"

Before anyone could stop her, Maddy waved her hand in front of the motion detector and the alarm screeched. The net fell from the ceiling and flattened Maddy to the floor. Screams of panic erupted. "Rosie, help!"

Nathan, Rosie, and Lucy ran to Maddy's side and pulled her free of the net. She stood shaking and quiet knowing she had made a mistake.

"Are you okay, Maddy?" Rosie wiped the dirt off of Maddy's cheek.

"Yes. Sorry, Rosie. It looked like more fun than that."

They all laughed and reset the trap – again. Rosie spread out a blanket in the clearing and they relaxed for a picnic lunch by the creek. Nathan skipped rocks and Maddy picked wild flowers. Rosie lie back on the blanket and let the sun warm her face.

Lucy gasped at the same time that Nugget bolted toward the trees. "I saw it! A red jacket."

They heard branches breaking and leaves rustling as something ran away. Rosie strained her eyes but could not see anything. Nugget barked but gave up the hunt.

Someone had been watching them. Hopefully their trap would keep Grymballia secure.

Chapter 8

Rosie lay awake in bed – again. She wished the cave alarm rang to her house, but since she didn't have a cell phone (because her parents lived-in-the-dark-ages), then the alarm went to Nathan. She worried that if Nathan's phone alerted an intruder, he would call Rosie's house phone, Rosie would charge into the forest to the cave, but she might be too late. The anticipation was killing her. She stared at her ceiling and Nugget shifted at the foot of her bed, also unable to sleep.

Flashes of a red jacket in the woods, her missing journal, and missing acorn necklace made her stomach swirl like she was on a merry-go-round. Rosie always turned in her homework assignments, her room was neat and tidy, and she knew exactly what T-shirt was in each dresser drawer. She didn't lose things. The thought of someone so mad at her to take revenge on her friends and family made her feel like she was in a horror movie.

She drifted off to sleep.

I stumbled through the ferns and tripped on a pile of dead mushrooms. Death and darkness surrounded me.

"Hello? Where is everyone? Spike? Jojo? Kimmie? Where are you?"

I walked around Grymballia, but nobody greeted me. The castle was silent and the villages empty. The gray sky hovered close to the ground in a haze and the air was cold.

Then, the screams. "He's gone! He's gone!" Goblet ran toward me, pale and panicked, with horror in his eyes.

"He is gone!"

Rosie bolted upright in bed, trembling. She glanced at her clock and it was 3:00 a.m. and she woke up Nugget with her dream. Nugget moved up closer to comfort Rosie. Her soft beard tickled Rosie chin as she rested her nose on Rosie's pillow.

Maddy burst into the room in a puddle of tears. "R-R-Rosie!" She huffed and tried to catch her breath between sobs. "G-G-Giblet!"

Rosie hopped out of bed and pulled Maddy into a hug. "It's okay, Maddy. It's okay. They're nightmares."

"But, Giblet!" Maddy's whole body shook as she cried.

"Shhhh. You're going to wake up Mom and Dad." Rosie pulled Maddy toward her bed and tucked her under the covers. Nugget curled up next to Maddy sensing that she needed her most. Maddy stopped crying.

She wiped away her tears. "Rosie, Giblet is gone."

The impact of Maddy's words punched Rosie in the gut. She had a similar nightmare, but Maddy stated it with such certainty. "It's just a dream, Maddy. We're going to protect Giblet and our friends."

Maddy shook her head violently. "It's too late. He's gone."

Rosie couldn't speak. Her sister did not have ESP or special superpowers, so how could she be so certain about Giblet? Rosie had nightmares, but she never woke up certain they were true. She hesitated asking Maddy more questions because she did not want to get her upset and crying again. They would never be able to explain it to their parents.

Rosie snuggled in next to Maddy as Nugget curled in a ball between them. It was only a nightmare – it was only a nightmare. Rosie convinced herself that Maddy could not tell her dream from reality, and they would have to be extra diligent in watching the cave for intruders. She dozed off and on, but sleep was useless. It was going to be a long day at school.

When Rosie climbed off the bus, she immediately searched for Nathan. Lucy caught up with her in the hallway.

"Yo, Rosalina Bobina, why are you in such a hurry?" Lucy found a different nickname for Rosie whenever possible.

Rosie continued marching down the hallway and barely paused. "We have to find Nathan and see if his cell phone alarm went off last night."

Lucy's face dropped and her joking demeanor disappeared. "What? Why?"

Rosie paused and said one word. "Nightmare."

"It must have been a doozy by the look on your face."

66

Nathan stood at his locker and Rosie and Lucy surrounded him. He smiled without looking concerned or worried. A good sign. "Hey, guys. What's up?"

"Did your phone go off last night? Any alarms?" Rosie leaned forward on her toes and searched Nathan for his phone.

Nathan furrowed his brow in confusion and grabbed his phone out of his back pocket. "I don't think so, why?" He typed in his passcode and then gasped. "Oh, no!"

Rosie grabbed her stomach. "What!"

Nathan flipped a button on the side of his phone. "My phone automatically goes to silent mode during the night. Why didn't I think of that?" He swallowed hard and pushed up his glasses. "It looks like it alarmed about 2:55 a.m. and I didn't know it." He groaned and looked like he might cry as his shoulders dropped in shame.

Rosie's legs tingled and felt weak and she held onto the locker for support so she didn't collapse on the floor. Nathan grabbed her shoulder. "Rosie, are you okay?"

She barely choked out the words. "The alarm sounded at the same time as our dreams."

Nathan and Lucy stared in silence.

Rosie relived her dream and heard Maddy's words in her head. Could Giblet truly be in danger? "I'm going to the cave."

The bell rang for first period.

Nathan shifted nervously. "Wait, right now? You can't miss the science test."

Rosie froze. Dang it. First period was a quiz they had been preparing for and it filled a large part of their grade in the class. She was torn.

Nathan gently tugged on her arm. "Let's make a deal. We'll take the Science test, and then we sneak out the back door before second period and run straight for the cave."

Lucy nodded. "Honestly, I could leave now because I didn't study anyway, but I'll follow you guys."

Rosie slowly walked toward class. "Okay." Images of Giblet filled her head. His cute green toothless smile and sucker drool running down his chubby belly. She sat in her seat in science class and was not sure she could concentrate on a test about proteins and amino acids.

The teacher, Mr. Koopman, shuffled papers and surveyed the classroom. "I hope everyone studied hard, because this test comprises a large part of your grade." He started to pass out the papers and then paused. "Where's Miranda?"

Miranda's desk sat empty.

Students looked around the classroom with empty stares and shoulder shrugs. Miranda had no close friends to ask her whereabouts. When a student was ill, Mr. Koopman usually had a report on his desk from the school secretary.

He continued passing out tests. "It's not like Miranda to miss a big test. She must be really sick or something important came up."

Rosie looked to Nathan who looked to Lucy who looked to Rosie.

Miranda was at the cave.

When Mr. Koopman reached Rosie's desk, she grabbed her test out of his hand and started answering questions immediately. It was a multiple-choice test and she knew the material well, but if she had the slightest hesitation to an answer – she chose C every time.

Typically after completing a test, Rosie would go over every answer two or three times to double check and use every minute of the test time, but today she whipped through it and sprinted up to Mr. Koopman's desk with her test in hand. "Done."

He glanced at the clock in shock. "Already?"

"I'm not feeling good, Mr. Koopman. Can I be excused?"

"Oh, okay Rosie. Stop by the office and they can give your parents a call."

Rosie turned toward the door and Nathan and Lucy looked up from their tests. Rosie could see that Lucy had only half of her test completed, but she stood up and strutted toward Mr. Koopman. "Here. I'm done."

Mr. Koopman looked over the test. "No, you're not done. Only half is completed."

Lucy squirmed and did a little dance. "I think I have diarrhea."

Mr. Koopman leaned back in his chair and his eyebrows went up.

Lucy hurried toward the door before he could ask any questions.

Rosie and Lucy stood in the hallway and covered their mouths to stifle their giggles. A minute later, Nathan walked out of the classroom.

Rosie whispered, "Nathan! I can't believe you left the test."

He shrugged. "I was pretty much done. Besides, we have people and worlds to save."

Lucy danced and wiggled for fun. "Did you tell him you have diarrhea, too?"

"No." A smiled filled Nathan's face and he scratched his head like a monkey. "I leaned over Mr. Koopman's desk and told him I was pretty sure I had head lice."

They cracked up laughing – silently.

Lucy paused. "Wait . . . do you?"

Nathan rolled his eyes. "Let's get to the cave."

Chapter 9

They sneaked out the back door of the school and dodged the janitor before he noticed their escape. They sprinted across the parking lot and Rosie threw her arms in the air feeling free and defiant as she skipped school. She never broke the rules and it felt . . . good. They jogged down the block and by the elementary school. Rosie stopped.

"Guys, I have to do something." Rosie walked toward the front doors.

"Rosie, you're going to get us caught!" Lucy yelled.

Rosie turned her head. "I have a plan."

Nathan and Lucy hid behind a tree as Rosie slipped inside the elementary school. Her heart raced as she looked around at picture books on shelves and crayon drawings on the walls. The front office had a doorbell outside of it to ring for entry. She pushed the button.

A gray-haired lady with pointy glasses attached to a chain around her neck shuffled to the door with a concerned look on her face. She pulled it open. "Well, hello. Shouldn't you be in school today?"

Rosie stood tall and took a deep breath. "I'm Rosie Montgomery, and I'm here to pick up Maddy for our grandmother's funeral today."

The sweet old lady's bottom lip stuck out and she wrapped her arms around Rosie's shoulders. "Oh, honey, I'm so sorry for your loss. I will ring Maddy's teacher to send her to the office right away." She grabbed the phone and after a few brief words she hung up. She turned again to Rosie. "Where are your parents, darling?"

Rosie had mentally prepared for this question. She dropped her eyes and stared at the floor. She blinked a lot because she couldn't fake cry on demand. "They're helping at Grammy's house because Grandpa is really sad and Grammy's cat won't stop throwing up since Grammy's gone."

"Oh, how dreadful."

The office door opened and Maddy walked in looking confused and shocked to see Rosie standing there. "Rosie?"

Rosie panicked and didn't want Maddy to ruin the charade. She grabbed her into a hug. "I'm here for you, Maddy. It's going to be okay."

"Huh?" Maddy squirmed in Rosie's arms but Rosie squeezed tighter and shuffled toward the door still holding Maddy in a bear hug.

Rosie nodded toward the secretary. "Thank you." She quickly turned to pull Maddy out of the office.

"Take care, dears." The sweet secretary called after them as they ran out the front door and down the sidewalk of the elementary.

Once they were a safe distance away, Nathan and Lucy came out from behind the tree. Lucy pumped her fist into the air. "Woohoo! Jailbreak. Rosie, you are on a roll today."

Maddy stomped her foot. "Rosie, why did I have to leave story time?"

Rosie leaned over to Maddy. "We're going to the cave, Maddy. We need to check to see if Giblet is okay. I thought you would want to come."

Maddy's eyes lit up and she threw her arms around Rosie. "Yes! Thank you."

Rosie knew they couldn't check on Giblet without his biggest fan. They walked between trees and ducked behind cars to the edge of town.

"Your house is about three miles out in the middle of nowhere." Lucy crossed her arms over her chest. "Exercise is not on my list of favorite things and I wore the wrong shoes." She held out her bedazzled boots with a pointed toe.

Nathan looked over the hillsides and put his hands on his hips. "Have you guys ever used Uber?"

Lucy laughed. "Do you think we live in the city? There's no Uber in a town this small."

Nathan pushed up his glasses. "Oh. I've heard my parents talk about it on their business trips."

Rosie couldn't waste time when they had miles to walk. She marched onto the county road leading out of town. "Maddy, stay off to the side so we don't get hit by a car."

Lucy groaned but reluctantly followed, and so did Nathan. The fall air was cool to allow them to walk a brisk pace with little effort. Rosie raced through many scenarios in her head as to what they might find in the cave. She hoped that a raccoon or rabbit tripped the alarm, but her gut told her otherwise.

Lucy limped and grabbed Nathan's shoulder. "My feet are killing me!" She stopped and pulled off her fancy boots. She had on pink fuzzy socks and she stood on the pavement. "That feels so much better." She continued walking in her socks.

Maddy followed quietly and said few words the entire three miles.

"Are you okay, Maddy?" Rosie asked.

She didn't look up and kept walking. "Giblet's gone."

Rosie glanced to Lucy and Nathan. "You don't know that. Giblet's got magic to protect him and he's smart."

Nathan asked, "What exactly did you two dream about last night?"

Rosie detailed the nightmares with Giblet missing and Maddy's certainty about Giblet's disappearance.

Nathan didn't say anything. The look on his face told Rosie he was worried.

They neared Rosie's house, and her mom's car sat in the driveway. They had to sneak around the house without being spotted – or they would be in DEEP trouble for skipping school. They devised a plan to walk past the house and hide behind the barn, and then they could cut through the trees instead of entering the forest on the main trail entrance.

"Dad said that's how we get poison ivy." Maddy said.

Rosie nodded her head. "Yep. We might."

Lucy put her boots back on.

They crept behind the barn and there was no sign of her mom in the yard or outside until . . .

BARK!

Nugget was outside.

She ran straight to Rosie and jumped onto her legs panting and dancing with excitement to see her in the middle of the day. Rosie bent down to rub her ears. "Nugget, shhhhh!"

Nugget quieted and licked Rosie's face.

"What do we do now?" Nathan said. "We can't put her back in the house or your mom will know someone is here, and if we take her with us, she will be looking for her."

Rosie was torn because she wanted Nugget to come with them into the forest, but she couldn't risk her mom searching for Nugget and finding them in the woods. She kissed Nugget on the nose. "Sorry, Nugget. You have to stay here and distract Mom."

Rosie had Lucy hold Nugget's collar while she slipped into the barn and grabbed a pile of rawhide dog bones. Each bone usually took Nugget an hour to chew, and Rosie grabbed three. "Nugget, it's your lucky day." Rosie launched the dog bones into the air and they landed in the middle of the yard. Nugget could not resist the chewy goodies as she chased after them and ignored Rosie as they snuck away into the forest.

They high stepped over the underbrush and weeds as it scraped their ankles and tickled their legs. Rosie already felt her legs itch and she wondered if it was because she was afraid of getting poison ivy. She pushed low-lying tree branches out of her face and held them up so they didn't hit Maddy walking behind her.

Lucy swatted the air and pulled leaves out of her hair as she groaned and grunted. "Why couldn't the entrance to Grymballia be hidden in a shopping mall?"

The trail surfaced ahead and they all gathered and brushed off their hair and pants. They looked up and down the trail and didn't see anything suspicious, so they hurried toward the clearing.

As they approached the break in the trees, Rosie knew something was different. She could not see or hear anything but she slowed her walking and held up her hands for the others to do the same.

"What is it?" Nathan whispered.

"I'm not sure," Rosie said. "Something's not right."

Silently, they stepped into the clearing. The creek tumbled quietly and no birds flew overhead. Rosie hoped she had overreacted. They hurried toward the cave.

Inside the cave was chaos.

The net piled on the dirt floor with nothing trapped underneath, and the motion detector lay in pieces scattered in every direction. Cold air surrounded them.

Rosie fell to her knees. "What happened?"

Nathan grabbed two fists full of his hair and pulled. "How could I have left my phone on silent!"

Lucy picked up fragments of the alarm system. "Something tells me that it wouldn't have mattered. Whoever did this was determined to get what they wanted."

Rosie scooped up the net and something fell onto the floor.

A note scrawled on lined paper:

I have your journal and I know your secrets. And now I have your little green friend. Take me to Grymballia, or I will use him to practice my science experiment.

Miranda

Rosie covered her mouth with her hand and gulped. Their worst fears were true.

"What does it say?" Maddy asked.

Nathan and Lucy looked to Rosie with big eyes that said *ARE YOU SURE YOU WANT TO TELL HER?????*

Rosie knelt down to Maddy. "Miranda took Giblet and we need to get him back."

Instant tears. "Why! Why did she take him? He didn't do anything to her."

"I know, Maddy." Rosie squeezed her hand. "Miranda is mad at me."

"And me, too for Ralph, the squirrel." Lucy added.

"And probably me for the science fair thing." Nathan shook his head.

Maddy wiped her tears. "I want Giblet back."

"We all do, Maddy." Rosie said.

Maddy wandered out of the cave to sit on the rocks, but Lucy, Rosie, and Nathan searched the cave floor for any clues. The mystery was how Miranda was able to get Giblet from Grymballia.

Nathan suddenly slapped his forehead. "She must have the acorn necklace, too!"

They surmised that Miranda destroyed the motion detector, but not before it alarmed Nathan. She tore down the net and called Giblet with the acorn necklace. When he came through the portal, she somehow grabbed him before he could escape or use magic. How she was able to do that - is a mystery.

"Where would Miranda take him?" Nathan asked.

"I have no idea. I think she lives out in the country not far from here," Rosie said.

Maddy charged into the cave screaming. "Rosie! Rosie!"

Rosie's heart sank. What could possibly have happened now?

"Look what I found between the rocks." Maddy held out her hand.

The acorn necklace.

Chapter 10

Rosie grabbed the acorn necklace out of Maddy's hand and screamed with joy. "You found the acorn necklace!" She looked into Maddy's proud eyes. "But how?"

Maddy pointed out of the cave. "I was sitting on a rock and using a stick to draw pictures in the dirt, but then I saw something shiny stuck between the rocks."

"I bet Miranda dropped it when she took Giblet," Nathan said.

"Nope. That's not what happened." Maddy rocked back and forth on her heels as she grinned.

Rosie had no clue what Maddy was talking about. "What do you mean?"

"Look what else I found." Maddy held up a root beer Dum-Dum sucker. "It's the special one I left for Giblet when we left Grymballia."

"Giblet somehow got the acorn necklace back from Miranda and left it for us!" Lucy cheered. "I love that little green man."

"I can't wait to hear his story after we rescue him." Nathan added.

Rosie hooked the acorn pendant around her neck and vowed never to remove it EVER AGAIN. They ran back into the cave. "We need to let Princess Nilly know what happened to Giblet."

"But Giblet is our key to getting into Grymballia. How can we get through the portal without him?" Lucy asked.

Maddy whimpered. "We need to go get Giblet."

"I know, but we need help. We have to try to reach Grymballia."

They gathered around the cave wall where the portal would appear. Rosie knew the chant that Giblet said every time they entered Grymballia. She rubbed the acorn and closed her eyes.

Land of the Earth, we have come forth,
We bear no harm and promise our worth.
Nature's our friend; we will never neglect
Grymballia we enter and always protect.

The acorn glowed and warmed in Rosie's hand. The familiar swirl of light glowed in the cave wall and a dark shadow moved toward them. They stepped back a few steps, uncertain of what or who to expect. Could Miranda have gotten into Grymballia?

The figure reached the portal entrance and they all breathed a sigh of relief.

"Goblet!" Rosie threw her arms around him. "We're so happy to see you."

Goblet's face looked strained and he didn't smile. "We must hurry to Grymballia. It's not safe." He pointed toward the portal.

They didn't hesitate and hopped through the spiraling bright light one by one. As they flopped into the cave on the Grymballian side, Goblet soon followed and sealed the portal. "Okay, now we can talk. I couldn't risk the intruder getting into the portal."

Rosie took a deep breath. "So you know about Giblet?"

Goblet dropped his head and kicked the dirt on the cave floor. "Yes. The Great Waterfall showed us."

Nathan squeezed Goblet's shoulder. "I'm sorry, Goblet. We'll get your brother back."

Goblet popped his head up and nodded. "We have been waiting for you to come to the cave. We couldn't risk coming to the outside."

"Somehow Giblet got us back the acorn necklace!" Lucy said.

Goblet smirked. "That sounds like my brother. We need to hurry to the castle. The others are waiting."

Rosie wanted to ask what they saw in the waterfall and who was waiting at the castle? She followed quietly and quickly behind Goblet as he scurried down trails and hopped over ferns. They traveled to the castle on foot, but sprinted almost the entire way. It ended up a similar travel time to Blim Birds.

When they reached the castle steps, Lucy collapsed and yanked off her boots. "Next time we're skipping school, hiking, running through Grymballia, and saving Giblet can you let me know in advance so I wear tennis shoes?"

Princess Nilly fluttered out the castle's front door darting back and forth. "Come inside. Come inside. We need to gather at the Great Waterfall." She disappeared into the castle.

Rosie sensed the urgency and knew Grymballia must be in danger.

Inside the castle, all of their friends greeted them. Princess Nilly didn't allow time for hugs and reunions and headed straight to the king's throne to turn the pinecone. The secret passageway opened up and she motioned for everyone to follow.

Tiki scooted up next to Rosie. "So good to see you, Rosie."

"Thanks, Tiki. Is everyone okay?"

Priscilla wore a sequined top hat and flipped a purse over one of her eight shoulders. "We were seconds from death, darling. Giblet sacrificed himself to that human monster to save us all."

Rosie gasped. "What do you mean?"

Tiki continued. "That person had your journal and read the portal chant as she rubbed the acorn necklace."

Rosie's face burned with embarrassment. It was all her fault.

Tiki continued, "She opened the portal, and if she would have entered Grymballia, we would all die and our world would disintegrate. Our magic would be discovered."

Priscilla stroked her long red hair. "But Giblet zipped through the portal and closed it again before she could get through."

Lucy had listened to everything. "Giblet is a hero."

Tiki and Priscilla nodded. "We owe him our lives."

When they reached the bottom of the stairs, the tranquility of Paradise Cove was overshadowed by Princess Nilly's urgency. Rosie wanted to smell the lilies and let a butterfly land on her finger to help her relax, but she knew it was not the time. Princess Nilly headed for the waterfall.

She raised her arms in the air and the waterfall parted mid-stream as it fell. The hidden passageway opened and everyone filed underneath the falls. Princess Nilly then closed the watery doorway and the thunder of the falls filled the room.

Rosie was surrounded by Maddy, Lucy and Nathan, but also by her Grymballian friends. The Glaperians Xena, Dina, Trina, Gina, Nina, and Patsy; and the Plumpians Spike, Dennis, and Rufus. Tiki and Priscilla stood nearby and Kimmie and Lila sprawled out on a rock. The Larmox: Sammy, Henry, and Jojo huddled together as a family while Goblet stood alone. Sid looked around often and Rosie suspected that she was looking for Nugget.

Princess Nilly spoke to the Great Waterfall:

Powerful water, we ask of you
To tell us what you see.
We respect your vision and your power
And will always protect thee.

Rosie was afraid of what the waterfall would show them. What might Miranda do to Giblet?

Princess Nilly addressed the crowd. "My friends, we haven't seen or heard from Giblet since he risked his life to protect us. Thankfully, Rosie and friends have come here to help once again. We must locate Giblet and bring him home safely, but keep the intruder out."

All of the Grymballia friends shifted anxiously on their feet or flippers. Others flitted about nervously in the air.

Princess Nilly turned toward the water and asked, "Great Waterfall, is Giblet okay?"

The water tumbled and roared but nothing appeared. Everyone stirred and looked to each other. Suddenly images appeared. Trees and a building with animals grazing outside.

Lucy whispered, "Are those sheep?"

The image changed and the building appeared to be a barn with its door wide open filled with animal pens. A person stood in the dim light.

Rosie filled with rage. "Miranda."

The image showed Miranda kneeling peering at something in the corner pen. As the image became clear, a scream went out and everyone gasped and pointed.

"Is that Giblet?" Jojo screamed. "What is she doing to him?"

Rosie continued to watch the scene on the waterfall. Giblet stood with his back pushed against a wall. His tiny arms were tied with shoestrings and he stood in a shallow pool of water. Aluminum foil wrapped around his tail that was tied to the wall with a string. Wires stretched everywhere connected to a black box with many dials. Miranda was talking to Giblet and waving Rosie's journal as she spoke.

"If I don't get to go to Grymballia, I'm going to connect you to my invention and your powers will be lost. If I plug these wires into this machine, then the electric current will flow into the water and then travel to your tail where the aluminum foil is wrapped. Your powers will be zapped away." Miranda cackled like a wicked witch from a Disney movie.

Giblet wiggled and tried to get free. His arms and tail pulled on the strings and his feet splashed in the water. But it was no use; he could not pull free. He did not look injured, but he did look furious.

The images in the waterfall were difficult to watch and soon Maddy started to cry. Her friend was a prisoner.

The image faded in the waterfall.

Kimmie and Lila slithered over to Maddy and rested their heads on her lap. Sid nuzzled her head on Maddy's arm and her pink curls tickled her cheek. Maddy was surrounded by others who cared about her and also loved Giblet.

When the image in the waterfall disappeared, Princess Nilly turned to the group. She no longer appeared nervous. She looked angry! The princess squeezed her tiny stick hands into fists and gritted her teeth as she flew back and forth while flapping her wings at record speed. "Listen up. We need to form a rescue team. Nobody treats Giblet that way."

Immediately, everyone started waving hands and volunteering to rescue Giblet.

"We can't send everyone out of Grymballia because we need guards at the portal to prevent Miranda from entering, and we need others to watch the waterfall for guidance. We can't risk being spotted on the outside world." Princess Nilly scanned the crowd.

"Can I poison the girl?" Kimmie asked as she rattled her tail back and forth in the air.

"You can use your powers, but you cannot kill Miranda. We're all angry, but she is a human and we will not take her life." Princess Nilly turned to Spike and shook her finger. "You cannot spike her." Spike scowled and rolled his eyes.

"This child is sad and lonely. Our goal is to rescue Giblet." Princess Nilly looked around again. "And bring him home safe."

Many Grymballians wanted to join the rescue mission. It took a lot of convincing from Princess Nilly to explain that guarding Grymballia was equally important to the rescue. They tried to choose the Grymballians with useful powers that would not be as noticeable in the outside world, and they also split up family groups.

The rescue team consisted of Nathan, Lucy, Maddy and Rosie. Spike lead with his expert battle experience and spikes. He could not use his poison, but he could still spike his opponent. Jojo, the Larmox, could burrow underground and fly. Patsy and Xena, the Glaperians, could see through objects and this ability always came in handy. Sid insisted on going and hoped to meet up with Nugget. Sid looked innocent with pink curls and frills but her mouthful of razor sharp teeth could shred a brick. Kimmie was ready to fight and her glowing power may be useful, and the final member of the rescue team was Priscilla. Her web-slinging abilities had proven valuable on many occasions. She packed her pink purse adorned with yellow flowers for the mission.

The guard team would remain and make sure that Miranda did not enter Grymballia. Goblet had to remain to guard the cave and to escort the group back and forth through the portal. Princess Nilly was going to stay in Grymballia to monitor the situation from Paradise Cove and the Great Waterfall. The remaining Grymballians on the guard team were Henry and Sammy, the Larmox; the Glaperians: Gina, Dina, Nina, and Trina; and Tiki, the water turk. Lila, the snake, was staying with Rufus and Dennis, the remaining Plumpians. The teams were formed, and they were ready to rescue Giblet.

Chapter 11

The rescue team rode Blim Birds to the cave. Rosie looked over her valiant team with amazing talents and knew they would see Giblet again soon. They gathered at the cave.

Rosie had something nagging her brain. "After we rescue Giblet, how do we keep Miranda from looking for Grymballia? She knows where the cave is and she knows about everything? She could just come back again." Her threat would never go away.

The King had escorted them to the cave and had been quietly observing while all plans were being made. "You are correct, Rosie. She will keep searching until she finds her way to Grymballia. We must help her forget."

Rosie didn't understand.

The king motioned for Rosie to follow him. "I have a plan."

The King approached a lush tree covered with fruit. Rosie remembered the juices exploding from the peaches they ate in Grymballia months ago. He pulled a peach off of the tree and held it in his hand.

Evil child that is a threat
Eat this fruit to help forget.
Another world you will not know
And never will you want to go.

He tapped the fruit with his index finger three times, it quivered for a few seconds, and then it looked like a normal peach again.

The king said, "Miranda must eat this peach after Giblet is rescued. She will forget about Grymballia and will never want to return here again." The King handed Rosie the peach.

Rosie gently took the peach and felt like she was being handed a priceless jewel. Her head spun. How do you make someone eat a peach? And what happens if she can't make Miranda eat it? She placed the precious cargo in her backpack and returned to the team.

Princess Nilly was to assure that the coast was clear on the other side of the portal as she watched from Paradise Cove. Princess Nilly would send a signal if she saw Miranda near the cave. They could not risk Goblet getting caught like his brother.

The cave filled with the entire rescue team.

"It's a party in here!" Lucy joked.

Kimmie flicked her tongue nervously. "I've never been to the outside world. I can't wait to see what it's like."

Lucy's eyes got big as she smiled. "You have Blim Birds and rainbows. We can't beat that in our world."

Rosie turned to the group. "We have to remember to avoid being seen." She glanced at the pink curly poof of Sid. If they ran into other people she would have to get creative with her storytelling.

Priscilla spun a web and was dangling from the cave entrance. She swung back and forth and kicked her hot pink boots in the air as her pink purse with yellow flowers dangled. She said, "Team, we're going to find Miranda and bring back Giblet."

"Yee-ha!" Spike yelled as his spikes shot out in every direction almost jabbing Lucy next to him. "Whoops!"

Goblet drew the sun on the cave floor while he chanted:

Land of the Earth, we must leave you now,
We keep all your secrets, we solemnly vow.
Nature's our friend and we will never neglect
Grymballia we now leave and always protect.

Rosie thought about the words that Goblet was chanting. They '*vow to keep the secrets*' of Grymballia. That was the most important part of their mission. They needed to make sure that Miranda did not find out about Grymballia. As the portal opened, Nathan jumped through followed by Lucy and then Maddy. The rest of the team leaped one at a time. Priscilla shot her web into the portal and then followed it as she floated into the air with legs flying. Kimmie hesitantly slithered into the opening but then Rosie heard her giggle as she took off. Jojo and the Glaperians flew through while Spike decided to curl into a ball and roll through the portal. Goblet and Rosie were left standing. Rosie hugged him tight.

"We'll find him, Goblet. I promise." Rosie slid into the portal.

The team gathered on the other side in the clearing by the stream. Miranda was nowhere in sight and the sun glowed bright on a crisp fall day. Patsy and Xena flew high and explored the treetops to assure nobody lurked nearby. Kimmie cruised in the grass admiring a world she had never seen. Priscilla weaved a web in a tree, and Jojo burrowed a tunnel and explored the underground. Spike stood next to Nathan, Lucy, Maddy and Rosie as they looked around.

"So we need a plan," Spike said. "Where do we find this Miranda person? We need to get Giblet away from that awful machine before it takes his powers."

"I agree," Nathan said. "Let's gather everyone."

Lucy shouted. "Everyone get over here!" Lucy was not afraid to use her outside voice.

Everyone gathered in a semi-circle and leaned in close to listen. Rosie kept looking over her shoulder worried that someone might be hiding in the trees. Sid did not hear anything with her impeccable hearing, so she assumed they were safe.

Rosie addressed the group. "The Great Waterfall showed Miranda holding Giblet in a barn. Miranda lives down the road on a farm not far from here."

"Do they have sheep?" Nathan asked. "It looked like sheep in the image."

"I'm not sure about sheep, but she definitely has lots of barns. Maybe Giblet is in one of those?" It made the most sense to check Miranda's house first.

"Let's go find out," Spike said.

The rescue team walked, flew, and slithered down the trail toward Rosie's house. Rosie suddenly stopped and looked at everyone.

"It will be fastest if we ride our bikes to Miranda's farm, but we have to sneak past Mom and Dad."

"I'm sneaky! I can get candy off the shelf and Mom never knows," Maddy said.

"What time is it?" Nathan said. "You both skipped school today. Won't they realize you didn't come home on the bus?"

Rosie tipped her head back and stared at the clouds. She totally forgot about the bus situation. Skipping school and being bad was difficult to coordinate and somewhat stressful.

Nathan looked at his phone. "It's 3:26 p.m."

Rosie grabbed Maddy's hand and sprinted down the trail. She yelled over her shoulder, "The bus will be here in two minutes! Meet us in the barn."

Rosie pulled Maddy and they ran until they had cramps in their sides and they panted like dogs. When they reached the backyard, Rosie paused. "I don't see them outside. Follow me."

They stayed low and followed the tree line around the edge of the yard. They ducked behind bushes and then hugged the side of the house. They turned the corner just as the bus whizzed by their house. "Come on." She tugged on Maddy's arm and they walked in the front door.

Rosie tried to catch her breath and act casual as if she just got home from school and not from a mile dead sprint through the forest. "Hi Mom, we're home."

Nugget sprinted around the corner and leaped into Rosie's arms. She sniffed her shirt and pants and whimpered. Nugget smelled Sid.

Her mom yelled from the kitchen, "Hello, girls! How was school today?"

Maddy looked to Rosie and giggled.

Rosie put her finger up to her mouth and leaned over to Maddy. "Shhh." Then she hollered to her mom. "It was fine. Do you care if Maddy and I go on a bike ride?"

Her mom appeared. "You just got home. Don't you want a snack or something?"

"Yes!" Maddy said instantly and Rosie wanted to kick her in the shins. They didn't have time for snacks, and a pack of magic Grymballians was hiding in their barn.

Her mom whirled around to the kitchen to get a snack.

Maddy shrugged her shoulders and whispered to Rosie, "I'm sorry, I'm hungry!"

"You need to eat fast because everyone is waiting for us."

Maddy held up her finger to Rosie with bright eyes. "I have an idea." She waltzed into the kitchen and asked Mom if she could take her snack on her bike ride.

Next thing Rosie knew, her mom was zipping open Rosie's backpack and putting food inside. "I packed snacks for your bike ride. You two have fun and watch yourself on the road."

"Thanks, Mom." Rosie lifted her backpack up and put her arms through the straps. "It's heavy! What kind of snacks did you put in here?"

"Fresh peaches. Have fun girls." She disappeared into the kitchen.

Rosie couldn't move. Her mom had placed peaches in her backpack, but Rosie already had a peach in her backpack – a magical peach to make someone forget Grymballia forever.

Which peach does she give Miranda?

Chapter 12

Rosie tried not to worry about the peach predicament for now while she and Maddy ran outside to meet the rest of their gang. She needed to concentrate on getting Giblet first. When they stepped off of the porch, she realized another crisis. Her dad stood talking to Nathan in the driveway.

Think fast. Think fast.

Maddy turned and ran back into the house for some reason, while Rosie approached Nathan. "Hey, Dad. You're home early." Her heart pounded out of her chest.

"I decided to come home and do a little yard work this afternoon. I didn't know your friends were coming home with you after school." He cocked his head to the side at Rosie.

Rosie usually needed permission to have friends over, so it was unusual for Nathan to suddenly appear at her house. Lucy waltzed out of the barn. "Hey, Mr. Montgomery," she said casually.

Her dad looked confused and turned to Rosie. Nathan had sweat beading up across his forehead.

Rosie babbled as fast as possible. "Lucy and Nathan rode home on the bus and we decided to go for a bike ride and mom said it was okay and Maddy and Nugget are going to come too. Do you like to ride bikes, Dad?"

Maddy came back out of the house pushing her baby stroller past Rosie and headed into the barn.

Rosie knew if she could get her dad talking about his childhood, he drifted off to la-la land and paid no attention to reality. "When I was a kid, my brother and I had bikes with banana seats and we put baseball cards in the spokes of the wheels . . ." he continued on and on and on.

Maddy pushed her stroller up next to Rosie and stood patiently. Rosie sighed a deep breath because Maddy insisted on bringing her baby dolls everywhere. But the baby blanket moved, and pink curls poked out from the stroller. Sid was hiding inside and Nugget paced at Maddy's feet.

Rosie's dad continued, " . . . One time when we rode up Baker's hill the mud was so thick that we got stuck. Our tires sunk so deep that Jasper had to jump off and run over to Oscar's house to help dig out our bikes." He laughed to himself. "Those were good days."

Rosie panicked that he would stop talking and notice Sid in the stroller, so she pushed him into more stories. "Did you ever fall off your bike, Dad?"

"Oh, yes! This one time I tried to jump over Rufus, our dog . . ." he continued.

Jojo popped up from the dirt between her dad's feet and realized how close she was, so she quickly burrowed back underground. Xena and Patsy flew high in the trees and Rosie caught sight of Priscilla sitting in a large web. The word "Shhhhh!" was woven in big print.

Rosie was about to burst. Sid in the stroller, Glaperians flying overhead, with Larmox under their feet while her dad was oblivious to it all. She interrupted him mid sentence. "Dad, we better get going on our bike ride."

He nodded his head. "I get to rambling sometimes. Have a good ride, and be careful." He turned and walked toward the house.

Lucy doubled over laughing. "That could be on Funniest Home Videos! Your dad had no clue that he was surrounded by Grymballians."

Kimmie slithered out from behind a rock where she had been hiding, and Maddy pulled back the blanket to reveal Sid sitting in the stroller wearing a baby bonnet. Spike had rolled himself into a ball and camouflaged himself between three rocks in the landscape. He walked toward the group, and they were all back together.

"That was close," Nathan said. "I can't believe he didn't notice everyone."

Rosie said, "I would say you all passed your first test of not getting noticed. We better get moving before our luck runs out."

They retrieved four bikes and helmets from the barn and rode toward Miranda's farm. Maddy's bike had a white Barbie basket on the front and Kimmie and Priscilla curled up inside. Priscilla spun herself a web in the basket to make the ride less bumpy. Patsy, Xena, and Jojo flew up above, while Nugget and Sid jogged along side of the bikes.

Spike didn't travel well. As a yellow ball with short legs, he couldn't keep up running aside the bikes and he didn't fit in the basket. Rosie decided to put him in her backpack. "Sorry, Spike. I think it's the fastest way."

Spike's eyes grew wide as he climbed inside the bag. "I think I'm getting a pretty good deal. Looks cozy."

Rosie could feel Spike rummaging around through all of her supplies. He yelled, "you have a lot of cool stuff in here!" Her bug spray flew out of the backpack. "Whoops!" Spike said as his head popped back up. "Didn't mean to do that. Thought I spotted some chewing gum."

Rosie shook her head and worried her bag was going to be destroyed. "Don't stick out your spikes or I won't have a bag left."

They rode down the road in single file and Rosie could barely keep up with Maddy as she powered down the road in the lead. She needed to get to her buddy, Giblet, and her legs were a pedaling frenzy.

Lucy rode in the rear on Rosie's mom's bike that didn't see much use. Its rusty handle bars left orange powder on her hands and the chain kept slipping off the track. The only good thing was the wide padded seat for extra comfort. Lucy said, "My butt is sure cozy, but you guys need to slow down! This rickety bike can only go so fast."

Nathan rode Rosie's dad's bike and it was a ten speed in excellent condition. He flipped to different gears and enjoyed the high tech equipment. Jojo, the Larmox, hopped a ride on the rack behind his seat. She had been burrowing for a while, but couldn't keep up. She decided to take a break and ride with Nathan.

"Did you bring any fancy weapons this time, Nathan?" Jojo asked. On the last rescue mission to Grymballia, Nathan brought weapons made of Diet Pepsi and Mentos to cause an explosion and also liquid nitrogen that froze the Fligarians until they crumbled.

"Not this time, Jojo. I'm not exactly sure what our plan will be if we run into Miranda. I hope we can talk some sense into her."

Jojo replied, "If she hurt Giblet, there won't be time for talking. She'll soon discover that Larmox aren't cute little flying worms."

Rosie frequently checked over her shoulder for cars and couldn't imagine what they looked like traveling down the road. Luckily, the road was quiet and not frequently traveled, and they had planned their strategy if a car would pass. Priscilla and Kimmie would duck down into Maddy's basket out of site, and Sid and Nugget would dive low into a ditch until the car passed. The crew flying overhead would avoid being spotted and hide behind telephone poles or trees. Spike hummed inside Rosie's backpack and rustled around.

They pedaled past two houses and Rosie's legs burned. She heard Lucy groaning from behind her. "Are we there yet?"

Maddy's lead was fading as she wore out, but all of a sudden she almost fell off her bike as she pointed and yelled, "Rosie, look!"

A flock of sheep grazed in a field beside the road. A large farm up ahead covered a vast amount of land with a farm house, multiple barns, a grain bin, and feed lots. They pulled over to the side of the road to discuss plans.

"That has to be Miranda's house," Rosie said. "We need to figure out which barn the sheep stay in so it will lead us to Giblet."

"We better figure out if Miranda is lurking around waving her pitchfork. We can't walk in and risk Giblet getting zapped," Lucy said. The others cringed at the image.

Nathan looked overhead. "Xena and Patsy, what if you fly ahead and use your special vision to check the barns. You might be able to see Giblet and see if Miranda is waiting inside."

Spike popped his head out of the backpack. "I have a slightly different plan. What if Patsy checks the house and Xena checks the barn? Then they can look for Giblet and Miranda at the same time."

"Great idea, Spike." Nathan said. "Xena and Patsy, do you think you can do that?"

"Sounds good. We'll find Giblet and Miranda, and then return here." They flew off.

"Let's get off the road. We'll store our bikes and gear in this field." Rosie lugged her bike off the road and laid it down in the long grass. "We don't want to be spotted by anyone passing and especially Miranda."

The sheep grazed peacefully munching in the field and would look up curiously at the mismatched crew walking toward them. Kimmie was fascinated by the sheep and couldn't wait to see one up close.

"They're so fluffy!" She giggled. "I want to snuggle on their back and take a nap."

Spike crawled out of the backpack and stretched his legs. He bounced around the field and shot his spikes in and out as he mumbled about something and staggered on his feet. He then was surprising quiet.

"Nathan, what was that machine that Miranda hooked up to Giblet?" Jojo asked.

"I'm not sure, but when she asked me to join her for a science project she talked about using electricity and magnets to produce energy. She's messing with a lot of potential power – and Miranda is smart."

Rosie's insides churned. She knew little about electromagnetic energy, but she had read enough to know that electromagnetic energy was the root of microwaves, X-rays, and ultraviolet radiation. Giblet was in grave danger.

Nathan continued. "If she hooks Giblet up to the wires on that box, the energy will transmit through the water and create energy that Miranda believes will take away his powers. I have no clue if it will, but I think it would hurt Giblet for sure." Nathan's face twisted with worry.

"We can't let her find out," Sid said. "We need to get Giblet out of there before she has a chance to try it out."

Spike was rolling around the field and watching the sheep. He turned to Lucy with a confused look. "Where am I?"

Lucy laughed. "You crazy little ball, you're in the middle of a sheep field."

"Oh, okay." He continued to roll around. Rosie assumed he could be getting dizzy from all of his rolling.

She watched the sky patiently awaiting the return of Xena and Patsy. Suddenly, Jojo popped up out of the dirt by her feet.

"Jojo, you scared me!"

"Sorry. I was out talking to the sheep," Jojo said.

Rosie squatted down and filled with excitement. "You can talk to them?"

"Yeah!" Jojo nodded. "But what does BAAA mean?"

Rosie smiled. "That's their special sheep language. I honestly don't know what it means."

Jojo glanced again at the sheep as they BAAA'd in the distance. "They don't have a very big vocabulary."

As Rosie watched the sheep, she caught glimpse of one resting on a pile of hay. On its back lay Kimmie, coiled up cozy and peaceful.

Xena and Patsy darted toward them over the field. "We found Giblet! He's in the second barn, which is the sheep barn. But Miranda is nowhere to be found." Xena sounded worried.

Rosie paced. "She wasn't in the house or in the barn?"

"No. We only saw Giblet hooked up to that dreadful machine." Patsy answered.

"If she's not there, then let's rescue Giblet before she comes back," Lucy said.

Nathan nodded. "It's risky, but we have to take the chance."

"We can't waltz onto the farm. How do we to get into the barn?" Rosie asked.

"BAAAAA," Jojo said. "We use the sheep."

"Brilliant!" Rosie hugged Jojo. "We can hide among the sheep and herd them into the barn."

Maddy had been sitting quietly with Sid and Nugget scratching their ears. "Rosie, is Giblet going to be okay?"

Rosie helped her up and squeezed her hand. "Let's go get him, Maddy."

Chapter 13

The sheep backed up slowly as the rescue team crept toward them. Rosie whispered, "Shhh, good sheep, good sheep." But it didn't help. They looked at her out of the corner of their eyes like she was a lunatic.

Nathan stopped. "They're too scared. Let's spread out and try to herd them toward the barn."

"But that doesn't help us hide with them?" Rosie said.

Kimmie stretched as she uncoiled from her resting place on top of her new sheep friend. "I can help." She slithered forward on the sheep's back and whispered into the sheep's ear.

The sheep stood up and belted out a loud "BAAAAAAA!"

The other sheep froze and turned toward Kimmie's sheep. They all gathered in a huddle with a medley of BAA's.

Jojo's mouth dropped open. "Fascinating."

Kimmie stretched tall on top of her sheep and turned to Rosie. "Follow us."

Her sheep led the flock as they followed on his heels. They no longer appeared scared of their group as Sid and Nugget trotted along at their feet and Priscilla shot a web from one sheep to another to form a swinging hammock as they traveled. Rosie, Lucy, Nathan, and Maddy hid between the huddled sheep so they were not spotted if someone appeared at Miranda's farm and they followed the flock as it waltzed toward their barn. Jojo burrowed underground, Spike rolled behind them, and the others flew overhead.

"Kimmie, you have sheep superpowers," Lucy said.

"I'm not sure I want to leave your world," she hissed. "It's amazing here."

They neared the barn, and Kimmie's sheep entered and the rest followed. Rosie scanned the farm yard and nobody was in sight. Jojo burrowed underground to avoid being trampled by sheep, and Priscilla flung her web up to the overhead wooden beams of the barn for safety.

Rosie listened closely to see if she could hear any movement and scanned down the length of the barn to assure Miranda was nowhere in sight. She could see Nathan and Lucy doing the same.

"I don't see anything, do you?" Lucy said.

The sheep stood together and stared curious as to what was so exciting in their barn, but now they were in the way. Kimmie whispered in her sheep-friend's ear and he led his flock into a corner to munch on their feed.

Xena fluttered, "Kimmie, the sheep whisperer."

Kimmie blushed. "Do you think my new friend could come back to Grymballia with us?"

A pile of dirt exploded in front of the group and Jojo appeared. "Did I miss anything?"

"We need to go this way." Patsy flew forward where they had spotted Giblet earlier. "I'm sure it was him that we saw in the corner stall, but it was really too dark to know for sure."

Maddy bolted forward to get to Giblet as soon as possible. She hollered, "I'm coming, Giblet!"

Nathan had been looking overhead and examining every inch of the barn when he grabbed Maddy's arm. "Stop! Nobody move."

Nathan looked up to the ceiling and Rosie followed his gaze. Dangling from a heavy rope was a heavy sandbag ready to fall directly on top of where they stood.

Lucy looked up and swallowed hard. "That can't be good. I could try to catch it, but I'm pretty sure it will crush me like a marshmallow in a s'more."

Rosie's eyes followed the rope attached to the sandbag across the ceiling and down the wall. It dropped across a wooden gate and stretched across the floor – one step in front of Lucy's foot. "Don't take a step, Lucy!"

Lucy spotted the rope and inched backward to get as far away as possible.

Rosie filled with anger. "Miranda set traps! She could really hurt someone."

Nathan shook his head. "She's smart. If she rigs the place, she doesn't have to stand guard of Giblet."

Rosie stood tall. "There's a reason she doesn't like me." Rosie took a wide step overtop of the rigged rope. "Because I'm smart, too."

Everyone carefully maneuvered over the rope and the sandbag stayed hanging overhead without crushing anyone.

"We have to be prepared for more traps," Kimmie said. "Let me slither ahead and see if I can see anything down at my level."

"We'll fly overhead and check it out from up here." The flying team of Patsy, Xena, and Jojo took off.

"Report back in five minutes." Nathan pushed up his glasses nervously.

Rosie wanted to sprint ahead and check on Giblet to see if he was there and if he was okay. She yelled down the barn stalls. "Giblet, if you can hear me, we're coming for you. Hang in there."

There was a faint sound from the other end of the barn.

Maddy screamed. "Giblet!"

Rosie grabbed her arm so she didn't bolt and run off after the sound.

"Was that Giblet for sure?" Lucy asked. "What if Miranda kidnapped other people? We've now established that she's loony-tunes."

"Giblet? Is that you?" Rosie yelled.

A louder noise came from the far end of the barn, but Rosie could not make out a voice or words. She took a few steps forward because it was hard to stand still.

Kimmie returned. "There are wires stretched across the path ten feet ahead. I can slide under them, but you would hit them easily. They are connected to some machine on the wall."

Nathan answered, "Trip wires. I bet they let Miranda know if someone is here. Good job, Kimmie."

"We can't let Miranda find out we're here." Rosie cringed at the thought.

Xena, Patsy, and Jojo returned. "Just before the last barn stall, there's a large net hanging overhead. Lights are shooting in different directions across the floor. We can see Giblet in the stall beyond that, but I can't see how we get past." Xena's voice strained and she sounded upset.

Rosie recognized what they described. "It sounds like a laser alarm. I bet if we hit one of the light rays, it triggers something." Her shoulder's slumped. "Does Miranda work for the CIA or something?"

Sid marched forward. "We'll find a way. Let's move forward, and Kimmie, tell us when we near the trip wires." Nugget panted and followed on Sid's heels.

Rosie realized how serious Miranda was about finding Grymballia by all the elaborate traps she had set. Kimmie glowed to light the dim barn and she motioned that the trip wire was close.

The thin wire was barely visible stretched across the barn floor. If Kimmie had not found it, Rosie knew Miranda would have discovered them in the barn. The wire was attached to a metal box on the wall with a green light glowing on top. They stepped carefully over the wire. Kimmie slipped underneath, and Rosie lifted Spike with his short legs overtop. Priscilla flew from web to web and avoided the floor altogether. Sid and Nugget hopped over with ease. Nobody tripped the alarm and another hurdle was accomplished. Now onto the laser show.

They stood at the end of the barn and neon yellow and green lights shot in different directions. The last corner stall lay beyond the lights, and Rosie knew that was where Giblet was held prisoner.

"Any ideas?" Rosie asked Nathan. He thrived on engineering and solving puzzles. Someday he would create magnificent things.

He pointed to the net overhead. "If we touch any of these lights, the net will fall on us." Nathan paced back and forth and examined the light beams. "Miranda knew to stretch the lights from the floor to the ceiling so that the flying and the crawling Grymballians were at risk."

"GEEEEZ!" Lucy groaned.

Nathan ignored her. "But I think that the lasers have to be generated by laser pointers and controlled by a radio device." He pointed to a pen-like gadget wedged between two barn boards. "If we break the circuit, I think the whole system will fall."

Rosie was amazed. "We just have to turn off the laser pointers?"

Nathan looked at me and shrugged. "I think so."

Lucy cocked her head to the side. "But the laser pointer is way over there." She pointed beyond the lights. "How can we get to it without triggering the trap and ending up in the big bad net?" Lucy sounded nervous.

"I'll do it." Priscilla said as she took off her hat and handed Jojo her purse to prepare.

Everyone turned to her. She was tightening the laces on her pink shoes and putting on fresh lipstick for the mission.

"Do you think you can dodge the lasers, Priscilla?" Nathan asked.

"Of course, darling. We'll be with Giblet in a few minutes."

She tightened a pink bow in her hair and then shot a stream of web into the air. Her web wrapped around a wooden beam overhead and Priscilla launched. Soon she was hanging from a web high above them and working frantically.

Maddy chewed on her fingernail. "Be careful, Priscilla."

The laser pointers were placed in opposite corners and the net hung overhead ready to fall if Priscilla nicked the light's beam. As they watched, she shot her web and then slid down a fine string between two beams of light.

"Priscilla, you could be an excellent jewelry thief." Lucy joked.

Priscilla concentrated as she reached the center of her strand and swayed back and forth as if she were teetering on a tightrope. She launched through the air with a flash of pink and landed on the laser pointer wedged in the corner. She dodged all the lights and she flipped off the power switch. The light beam turned off.

"Woohoo! Way to go Priscilla!" Xena and Jojo and others cheered.

"Wait, why didn't the whole system shut down?" Rosie turned to Nathan.

He ran his fingers through his hair. "We must have to turn off more laser pointers."

Priscilla wasted no time and shot a web up to the next wooden beam. She flew into the air and double-flipped as she slipped between two beams of light on her way. She weaved a web and planned her next move as she examined the next laser pointer below.

Rosie knew that Priscilla was the best web-slinger around, but she did not expect what she saw next.

Priscilla removed her pink boot and spun a coil of web around it. Then she used a rope of web and swung her pink boot overhead like a lasso and launched it toward the laser pointer.

Direct hit!

"Whoa!" Spike yelled. "You hit the power switch!" The laser shut down and the light went out.

She pulled her boot back up to her web, rubbed off a speck of dirt, and then slipped it back on a foot.

Two laser lights had been shut off, and then it triggered a chain reaction. The remaining laser lights flickered and flashed, and then they all turned off.

"It worked!" Nathan yelled.

The net did not fall and the laser beam alarm was shut down. Priscilla scurried down the barn pole and she was raised in the air like a champion.

Rosie looked forward to the dark, dreary corner stall of the barn. "Let's get Giblet!"

They hurried to the corner and pulled open a rickety wooden door that blocked the entrance. As Rosie pulled it open, they heard a noise.

"Giblet?" Rosie stopped and her gut told her to use caution. It didn't sound like Giblet.

Maddy pushed the door open and rushed inside.

And then she screamed.

Chapter 14

"Giblet! Giblet!" Maddy ran to his side.

Giblet appeared frail, weak, and his color was gray. He stood propped up in six inches of water hooked to multiple wires with his tail wrapped in aluminum foil. His mouth was taped shut and his eyes were wide and face shaking as he tried to talk.

"Wait, Giblet. Let me get the tape." Rosie hurried forward and gently removed the tape. Giblet's green, smooth skin was now dry and cracked and wanted to tear as Rosie tugged on the tape. "I'm so sorry, Giblet. I'm not trying to hurt you."

After one of his hands was freed, he grabbed a corner of the tape and ripped it off in one swoop. "Ahhhhh!" He yelled and then licked his sore lips. "That feels much better."

"Giblet, are you okay?" Rosie asked.

"I am now." Giblet said with a big toothless smile. "I've never been happier to see you guys. Especially you." He squeezed Maddy's cheek.

Maddy helped Giblet out of the water and his green toes were wrinkled. Nathan pulled off the wires and aluminum foil, and then Maddy threw her arms around Giblet for a solid minute.

"Did Miranda hurt you, Giblet? Do you still have your powers?" Jojo asked.

"I have my powers, but Miranda would have taken them soon. She wants to get into Grymballia."

Rosie nodded. "We know. I'm so sorry, Giblet."

Giblet squinted his eyes and Rosie saw his anger. "She tricked me at the cave."

"It's not your fault, Giblet. It sounds like you saved everyone in Grymballia by offering yourself instead," Rosie said. "You're a hero."

Giblet kicked the barn floor with his wrinkled foot. "No, I'm not."

Jojo and Priscilla chimed in. "You are, Giblet! You saved us."

"We need to get back to Grymballia before she comes back, then we'll be safe." Lucy said.

Giblet didn't move. "She'll keep coming. She knows our secret."

"The King came up with a plan to solve that." Rosie pulled a peach out of her backpack, but not certain if it was the correct one. "If we can get Miranda to take a bite of the magic peach, she will no longer remember Grymballia."

Giblet smiled a wide, toothless grin and his gray gradually turned to green before Rosie's eyes.

"Let's go, gang." Sid motioned and everyone followed.

Rosie sprinted through the barn, and then realized their mistake. "Stop!"

But it was too late.

Lucy fell to the floor after her shoe caught the trip wire. The green light on the wall monitor alarmed and started flashing red.

"Oh, no!" Rosie yelled. "Miranda will know we have Giblet. Run!"

Rosie helped Lucy up and they remembered to dodge the rope holding the sandbag. They flew past the sheep, but Kimmie paused a moment to say good-bye to her new friend.

Without looking back, they powered across the field to where their bikes were hidden in the long grass. Rosie scooped up Spike and tucked him inside her backpack again. Kimmie slithered through the grass with Priscilla riding on top in a webbed saddle. Maddy ran with Giblet tucked in her arms, while Nugget and Sid ran panting beside them. Jojo burrowed underground and Patsy and Xena flew overhead.

They hopped on their bikes and pedaled frantically. Rosie looked over her shoulder expecting to see Miranda chasing after them on her broomstick. Where was she? Rosie pedaled faster knowing she needed to get her friends back to Grymballia.

Spike peeked his head out of her backpack. "Where are we going?"

"Home." Rosie said.

"Where's home?" Spike said innocently.

Confused, Rosie looked over her shoulder at Spike and suddenly lost control of her bike. She fell into the ditch.

"Rosie, are you okay?" Lucy hurried to her side.

Rosie grabbed her backpack and unzipped it wide open. She looked down inside at Spike snuggled in with the peaches.

The peaches!

"Spike, did you eat a peach?" Rosie's heart pounded.

"No."

"Oh, thank goodness." Pure relief filled Rosie.

"Well . . . I didn't eat a whole peach."

Rosie stared at Spike but she couldn't speak.

"I spiked each peach and tried a sample of each one." Spike grinned a dopey smile.

Rosie flopped backward in the grass and stared at the sky.

Nathan leaned over her. "Did you hit your head when you fell off your bike?"

Rosie shook her head. "I'm fine." She slowly stood up. "But Spike's not."

"What do you mean?" Nathan said as he stared at Spike sitting in the backpack.

"Spike took a bite of the King's magic peach. He doesn't remember Grymballia."

"What!" Jojo popped up out of the dirt and peeked into the backpack. "Spike, what do you mean you don't remember Grymballia?"

Spike tilted his head at Jojo. "Grym –what?"

Jojo flitted her wings and lifted into the air. "This is a crisis. We need the King to fix this."

Rosie pulled her bike out of the ditch, checked that Spike was cozy in her backpack, and then zipped it up again. "We have to get to the cave or Miranda is going to find us. Hopefully, the King can help Spike if we can get him there soon."

Rosie couldn't believe she had messed up again. What if Spike couldn't remember? She pedaled harder than if she was being chased by a

Fligarian, but also because everything was happening so fast. She still had to figure out how to get Miranda to eat the magic peach, and she still didn't know which one it was! She knew the peach worked since Spike's memory was zapped. If only he had sampled only one peach instead of all three.

"My chest, legs, and aching feet are going to explode if I stay on this bike much longer." Lucy's red face poured with sweat.

"We're almost there." Rosie saw her house up ahead and scanned the yard to see if her parents were outside. She couldn't see anyone. "Kimmie and Sid, take your crew behind the barn and we'll meet you out back as soon as we can."

Rosie, Nathan, Lucy, and Maddy pulled their bikes into the barn and tried to be quiet so they didn't draw attention from the house. As they walked out of the barn, Rosie's mom stood there to greet them.

"Hey, kids. Did you have a good bike ride?" She looked from face to face. "You guys are filthy."

"It was fun. I think we're going to hike out to the clearing in the forest." Rosie casually walked past her mom like it was no big deal. She feared that if she asked permission, her mom might say no.

"Just be careful. You're going non-stop today." Luckily, she headed back toward the house.

"Thanks, Mom." Rosie pulled Maddy's hand.

In the backyard, Rosie saw Nathan and Lucy waiting by the trail at the edge of the forest. After another glance over her shoulder to assure her mom and dad were nowhere in sight, Rosie said to Maddy, "Come on, let's hurry."

Sid and Nugget chased each other around trees and Priscilla dangled from a new web hanging from an overhead branch. Maddy ran up next to Giblet where he rested on a rock.

"Giblet, I was so worried about you. I had bad dreams that you were hurt." She sat next to him and scooted as close to Giblet as she could without bumping him off the rock.

"Thank you for rescuing me." Giblet looked to Maddy and then turned to Rosie and the others. "I can't imagine what might have happened if you didn't get there when you did."

Rosie couldn't bear to think about it. "Thank goodness you still have your powers, Giblet."

"We'd better get going. We don't know where Miranda is, and since we tripped her alarm, she knows that Giblet is gone." Nathan looked over his shoulder and scanned the forest. "We have to watch our backs."

They hiked down the trail and continuously looked through the trees and beyond the trail. Suddenly, every bird's tweet or leaf's rustle sounded suspicious for someone sneaking up behind them. Rosie glanced at Spike trotting alongside the group. His eyes were glazed and he looked up into the sky with a goofy smile, oblivious to where they were going. Rosie closed her eyes and shook her head, frustrated that she didn't think of the peaches in her bag when she offered to give Spike a ride. Hopefully, the King could help fix Spike's memory.

Kimmie slithered and watched for Miranda from the forest floor, and Jojo burrowed underground. Xena and Patsy scanned the sky above.

Nugget bolted forward and barked with her hair standing on end as she stared into a cluster of trees. Sid immediately stood at her side growling and baring her ferocious teeth.

"What is it, Nugget? Sid? What do you hear?" Rosie whispered, and then laughed internally that she expected her dog to answer her questions. She had been around Grymballians too long.

"Xena, can you fly ahead and scan the area? Stay hidden so you're not spotted. Look through the trees if you need to." Rosie asked.

"I'm on it." Xena flew up, up, and away.

Rosie squeezed her fists and shifted her feet in the dirt as she waited anxiously. Nugget and Sid stood pointed at the same spot letting out low growls. Rosie heard a rustle in the bushes a short distance ahead, but could not see anything. A pile of dirt burst up at her feet.

"Jojo! Dang it!" She had to quit doing that.

"There's someone on the trail!" Jojo whispered. "When I was underground, I felt a new vibration up ahead on the trail. I hurried back here to warn you."

"Good work, Jojo." Rosie pointed to Nugget and Sid. "I think it's over there. Xena is checking it out."

Sid growled and the bushes rustled. A flash of movement caught Rosie's eye.

Xena came zipping back with many wide panicked eyes. "It's Miranda! Hide, quickly! She's coming this way."

Everyone ducked into a nearby shrub or hid behind a tree. Jojo dove underground, Kimmie hid under a rock, and Priscilla clung to a branch. Lucy scrambled to find a spot in a panic.

Giblet jumped in front of the group and smacked his tail three times. Sparks flew and he waved as he whispered, "I used the invisibility spell. We should be covered for a short period, but she can still hear us. Be very quiet."

Rosie remembered the invisibility spell when they hid from the Plyrim soldiers in Grymballia. It wore off as Nathan was walking by the soldiers and he narrowly escaped. Hopefully, the spell would hold until Miranda was gone.

The rustling in the bushes grew louder, and out stepped Miranda in a red sweatshirt. It was hard to remain calm when anger, fear, and frustration coursed through Rosie's body. She had the urge to charge up to Miranda and tell her what she thought of her torture of Giblet. But Rosie stood frozen – and watched.

Miranda frantically looked under plants and up into treetops. Rosie knew she searched for Giblet. Miranda had dark rings under her eyes and her hair shot out in ten different directions. Her usual manicured appearance was now a frazzled, tired mess. She carried a grape flavored Dum-Dum in her hand to lure Giblet out of the trees.

Maddy gasped and squeezed Giblet's hand. Rosie noticed Giblet's big eyes and touch of drool.

Miranda stopped and looked around with furrowed eyebrows and squinted eyes. She had heard Maddy's gasp but could not figure out where it came from. Maddy held her hand over her mouth and shook her head at Rosie with big eyes to say she was sorry.

After sitting silent for what seemed like an hour, but was only about two minutes, Miranda's shoulders slumped and she sat down on a tree stump. She was only five feet away from their group, so they were trapped and could not move. Rosie hoped their invisibility spell lasted long enough. Then Miranda did the most surprising thing . . .

. . . she cried. She dropped her head in her hands and tears fell as she sobbed. As she wiped her eyes, she said, "What have I done?"

Rosie was caught off guard by the monster acting human. Did she regret what she had done to Giblet? She glanced to Lucy and Nathan, and their faces proved that they were equally confused by Miranda's tears. As Rosie looked at Lucy, she saw that her arm was becoming visible.

Rosie pointed frantically, yet quietly, to Lucy's arm and she stepped behind a tree. What could they do? They were about to appear right in front of Miranda's eyes.

Nathan picked up a small rock and tossed it far down the trail behind them. Miranda heard the noise and jumped up from her seat. She paid no attention to the shadow of figures appearing around her as she ran down the trail toward the sound. She almost stepped on Maddy's toes as she sprinted past.

Nobody moved for another minute until Miranda was far enough away. Then Rosie let out a huge sigh of relief. "Whew! That was too close."

Lucy leaned over with her hands on her knees. "I thought I was going to have to use my karate moves if we appeared in front of Miranda." Lucy held up her hands in a karate chop stance.

"You know karate?" Nathan sounded impressed.

Lucy shrugged her shoulders. "Well, no, but I have watched the Teen Karate Ninja movie at least fifteen times, and I think I have the moves mastered."

Nathan rolled his eyes but couldn't help smiling.

They all became fully visible as they hurried down the trail toward the clearing. Rosie wanted to sprint, but knew everyone could not keep up if she did. Miranda would return soon. As soon as they entered the clearing, Rosie pointed. "Everyone to the cave."

Spike stopped. "What cave?" He had been following the crowd until now, but had no idea where they were going or why.

Rosie's stomach dropped to her toes. She knelt in front of Spike. "Your home is on the other side of this cave, Spike. It's called Grymballia."

Spike's face filled with shock. "What are you talking about?" He looked up and around at the trees and then back to Rosie with confusion. "Don't I live here?"

"We have to hurry, Spike. It will all make sense soon. I promise."

Everyone squeezed into the cave and constantly checked the entrance for Miranda. They could not risk her getting into Grymballia, or their world would be destroyed.

"We need to hurry!" Lucy said in a panic.

"But if we go, we still need Miranda to forget about Grymballia." Nathan looked to Rosie. He knew she had the peaches and the difficult task she was given.

"We need to get everyone out of here first so that nobody else gets hurt." Rosie said. "Giblet, can you take us home?"

Giblet smiled his toothless grin. "I can't wait."

Spike looked scared and confused.

Giblet scratched the sun into the cave floor. Everyone scrunched together to make room and then he started the chant:

Land of the Earth, we have come forth,
We bear no harm and promise our worth....

"I found you!" Miranda stood at the cave entrance holding a large stick.

Chapter 15

"Miranda!" Rosie instinctively stepped in front of Maddy, Giblet, and the other Grymballians to protect them.

Miranda's eyes squinted and her lips pursed as anger filled her face. She was no longer the crying, sad girl they saw moments earlier. Rosie wondered what happened to her remorse and guilt. Miranda said, "You can't go to Grymballia without me. I'm coming too."

Rosie stared at the large stick that Miranda waved wildly in the air. "Miranda, calm down. Don't hurt anyone."

Nathan added with his hands in the air. "Please put the stick down."

Miranda flashed surprised and embarrassed eyes to Nathan. She had a crush on him and now she had made herself look bad.

Miranda stammered, "W-w-well, how do I know these freaky animals (she pointed to Sid and Spike) won't rip my face off?"

Lucy stepped forward and smirked. "They might."

Rosie added. "They could if you hurt them. But Miranda, look what you did to Giblet! That was horrible!" Rosie gritted her teeth and clenched her fists.

Miranda took a step backward and raised her stick in the air. The Grymballians responded to her threat and erupted in a clash of energy. They were face to face with the monster that tortured Giblet.

They attacked.

Priscilla had been hanging quietly close to Miranda' head, and she shot out a web and snagged Miranda's stick. It flew out of her hand and onto the floor.

Miranda ducked her head and screamed, "What was that?" She looked around trying to figure out what had happened.

Xena, Jojo, and Patsy flew toward Miranda's face. She charged at the flying creatures, but then caught site of Xena and Patsy's multiple eyes and Jojo's worm-like Larmox body. She panicked and fell over backward onto her behind. Kimmie glowed bright in the dim cave and slithered up Miranda's leg.

Rosie worried about Kimmie's anger. "Remember, no poison Kimmie!"

"POISON?" Miranda kicked her leg trying to push Kimmie away.

Spike rolled next to Miranda and shot out his spikes. He might not remember Grymballia, but he knew Miranda was the enemy. Sid and Nugget attacked with ferocious growls and Sid flashed her razor sharp teeth.

"STOP! STOP! Please stop. I-I-I was not going to use the stick." Miranda sobbed. "I don't want to hurt anyone. I only took your green friend to get your attention, I wasn't going to hurt him." She turned to Giblet. "I'm sorry. I read Rosie's journal and just wanted to be part of the big secret."

Rosie had a moment of sympathy, but then her brain returned to the multiple traps Miranda had left in the barn and the image of Giblet pinned down to the machine. She had an idea. If she could get Miranda away from the cave, then the Grymballians could sneak back through the portal safely. She rested her hand on her backpack. She still needed to figure out which peach was the magic brain-eraser.

"Miranda, let's talk about it. How about you come out to the clearing with Lucy, Nathan, and me, and we'll tell you as much about Grymballia as we can."

Lucy turned to Rosie with crazy face. "What?!"

Rosie winked to indicate she had a plan.

Miranda crossed her arms over her chest. "Why should I trust you?"

"Miranda, these creatures wouldn't mind wrapping you in a web, spiking you, turning you into water, and Giblet has powers you cannot even imagine. You hurt their friend." Each of the Grymballians glared at Miranda. Rosie continued, "The cave is not a safe place for you right now. You can come with us, or you can meet Spike."

Spike rolled around in a circle three times, flew into the air, and then bounced onto his feet covered in spikes. He rested a long spike next to Miranda's big toe. She took a step backward.

"Okay." Miranda kept her eyes on Spike. "But I'm coming back in here afterward to see where this cave leads. I saw the green guy come from a hole in the wall, and I know how to use this necklace." She grabbed at her neck. When she didn't feel the acorn necklace her face fell in shock. "Where is it?"

"You mean this necklace?" Rosie touched the acorn where it dangled around her neck.

Maddy chimed in. "Giblet got it. Haha!"

Miranda's shoulder's slumped in defeat. "Okay, let's talk."

Miranda led the way out of the cave, but before Rosie stepped out, she whispered to the Grymballians and Maddy, "Hurry, go to Grymballia! We'll distract Miranda. Maddy, stay with Giblet and take Nugget. I'll meet you soon."

Maddy grabbed Giblet's hand and pulled Nugget close to her side. "Okay, Rosie."

Rosie knew Giblet would take good care of them.

Giblet chanted:

...Nature's our friend; we will never neglect
Grymballia we enter and always protect.

As Rosie stepped out of the cave into the sunlight, she heard Giblet smack his tail and she knew the portal would open and they would soon be safe in Grymballia.

Now to protect them from Miranda.

Chapter 16

Nathan and Lucy led Miranda far away from the cave and over to the stream. She was sitting on a boulder with her arms still crossed over her chest and a distrusting look on her face.

"You guys better start talking, or I'm going back into the cave," Miranda said. "I'm not scared of those little monsters. I can find another stick." She waffled as she spoke and her eyes looked off toward the forest. Rosie knew she was nervous and scared. Seeing Sid's teeth and Spike's points, and being attacked by Kimmie and Priscilla had to be terrifying. Rosie was happy they were on the same team.

Nathan started. "Why are you doing this? You have to quit being so jealous of Rosie and stop hating her so much."

"I am NOT jealous of HER." Miranda could not look at Rosie.

Nathan acted as referee and positioned himself between the two of them. Lucy stood next to Rosie to make her support clear. Lucy barked back immediately to Miranda. "You're constantly competing with Rosie! Every test or project you compare yourself with Rosie. When she beats you, you take it personally and blame her!"

Nathan talked calmly. "Miranda, you're incredibly smart, and so is Rosie."

Rosie stared at the grass. She'd never heard Nathan talk about her like that before.

Nathan said, "If you actually worked WITH Rosie, just think what you two could accomplish!"

What? Rosie had never thought about that before. She glimpsed at Miranda and they met eyes. They both quickly looked away.

Miranda put her head down and did not speak right away. "I've made a mess of everything. You guys are always laughing and having fun and passing notes." She glanced to Lucy. "When Nathan didn't want to be my Science fair partner, I got super angry."

"You think?" Lucy tapped her foot.

"And YOU killed Ralph!" Miranda snapped at Lucy.

"I did not!" Lucy stomped her foot, but then stopped herself and took a deep breath. "Look, Miranda, I'm sorry about what happened to Ralph. I liked that little furry rat, too."

Miranda looked from Lucy to Rosie. "I hid in the bathroom stalls and heard you guys talking, and then I stole your journal." Miranda's face twisted. She reached into her bag and pulled out Rosie's journal and handed it to her. "I wanted to go with you guys and see Grymballia. You make it sound so wonderful."

"But why do such mean and creepy things?" Lucy said.

"I've been working on my electromagnetic energy project for months, and I figured out how to use it to pop open your locker and steal the notes you pass in class." She dropped her eyes with guilt. "I read about Giblet and that he was the key to

Grymballia. I thought I could use him to get your attention."

"How about sending a text message next time," Lucy said.

Everyone shared a small laugh.

Nathan leaned forward. "Is the electromagnetic machine your science fair project?"

"Yes," Miranda answered. "I can produce energy with magnetism, and I have different devices to power up with my box."

"It looked like Frankenstein – mad scientist stuff. It was horrible to see Giblet hooked up. How do you know about that kind of stuff?" Lucy asked.

"Energy amazes me. I do a lot of research and my dad has all kinds of computer parts around the house that I used to help build it," Miranda explained.

"I have an idea, Miranda." Rosie turned to Nathan briefly. "If it's okay with you, what if we combine our science projects? Nathan and I are using solar power for energy. What if we make a big display on which energy type is more efficient? It would blow everybody away!" Rosie envisioned their project making it to a national level.

Miranda and Nathan's eyes grew wide and excited.

"What a great idea!" Nathan said. "If we put our heads together, we could make such a great project."

"That's way too much brain power in the same room. You might blow a fuse." Lucy joked.

"You guys would work with me?" Miranda asked with surprise in her voice.

"Sure. If you stop torturing our friends," Rosie said.

"Deal. Are you going to tell me about Grymballia?" Miranda asked with hesitation.

Rosie twisted with a tough decision. Obviously their relationship with Miranda was mending, but they could not risk Grymballia and the lives of their friends. Rosie didn't feel she could fully trust that Miranda wouldn't still want to GO to Grymballia once she heard about how wonderful it was. She had to think fast.

"Grymballia is a magical place, but if you were to enter Grymballia they would all die and their world would disappear."

Miranda's face showed pure horror. "What! Why?"

Rosie continued. "Because you are from the outside world, they cannot risk Grymballia being discovered and their people threatened."

"But I would never tell anybody."

Lucy chortled.

"I wouldn't!" Miranda said defensively.

"Grymballia is filled with rainbows and waterfalls, and their world is run on solar energy. They feed everyone naturally with the food grown in their own soil and the creatures are fantastic." Rosie envisioned Grymballia as she spoke.

"Your journal talked about a King and Queen?" Miranda leaned forward and soaked up every word.

Rosie squirmed. She needed to stop giving details. If she chose the wrong peach for Miranda, then she would not forget Grymballia. "How about a snack? My mom packed fresh peaches."

"I'm starving."

Rosie opened her backpack and gazed at the three peaches resting in the bottom. One of them Spike had stabbed and it erased Grymballia from his mind forever. They all looked the same when Rosie grabbed the peaches. She glanced to Nathan and Lucy. "I only have three." She looked to them with big eyes that said: DON'T EAT A PEACH!

"I'm not hungry," Nathan said.

"I hate peaches," Lucy stuck out her tongue.

It was a game of chance to see if Rosie chose the correct peach. One of the three peaches would wipe Grymballia from Miranda's mind. She needed to be sure that Miranda ate it, so Rosie decided to increase the odds. "I love peaches. I'll eat one with you."

Lucy squeaked. "Rosie! I thought you hated peaches. I thought you barfed with peaches! You can't eat a peach."

Miranda looked at Lucy like she was nuts.

Rosie examined the peaches in her bag and listened to her gut as to which two she should grab. She slowly handed a peach to Miranda.

Rosie turned to Lucy. "I like peaches, but some are sweeter than others."

Miranda immediately chomped a huge bite out of her peach and juices ran down her chin.

Rosie, Lucy, and Nathan stared at her. Waiting. How would they know if it was the magic peach and if she forgot Grymballia? They couldn't risk asking her about it or she would start asking questions. Maybe the magic took a while to kick in?

Miranda continued to eat her peach. "When did you discover Grymballia?"

Rosie panicked. Does that mean Miranda did not have the magic peach or that she needed to eat more? Rosie stared at her own peach. What if hers was the one to wipe her memory of Grymballia.

"You're not eating your peach? They're so good." Miranda took another bite. "Eat some."

Miranda looked at Rosie curiously as to why she was not eating her peach. Rosie put the peach up to her mouth and opened her mouth. She heard Lucy let out a slight gasp and Nathan shift on his heels. Rosie's mind flipped through images of her Grymballian friends, riding through rainbows, battling Plyrim soldiers, and walking through the beautiful castle. She knew she had to protect her friends and their world.

Rosie bit into the peach.

She chewed and struggled to swallow not knowing what might happen. She did not feel magic surging through her body and the peach tasted delicious. Nathan and Lucy stared with wide eyes, and Rosie shrugged her shoulders.

"Aren't they great?" Miranda devoured her peach practically to the pit.

Rosie nodded her head and felt numb. She tried to keep images of Giblet, Goblet, Blim Birds, Franklin, and all of her friends running through her head to keep them from disappearing. Her heart raced and she filled with fear at possibly losing the most important thing that had ever happened to her. She wiped the juices from her chin.

Suddenly, Miranda stood up, gathered, and packed her things.

Rosie, Nathan, and Lucy could only watch with curiosity.

"Thanks for having me out here today. This was fun. I can't wait to combine our science projects. Maybe we can talk about it more next week. I better get going or Mom will worry about me." Miranda walked toward the forest trail. "Bye, guys." She waved and walked away.

"Uh, bye," Nathan said.

"See you, Miranda," Rosie said. Miranda asked no more questions about Grymballia and had no desire to enter the cave. "It worked!"

Rosie leaped into the air and took another bite of her safe peach.

"You're nuts, Rosalina Montgomery!" Lucy put her hands on her hips. "What if you had chosen the wrong peach?"

"I had to try. If she didn't trust me, she wouldn't have eaten the peach."

Nathan shook his head. "Amazing. You had a 33% chance of choosing the correct peach, how did you know which one was the magic peach?"

Rosie thought about it. How did she explain her gut feelings that guided many of her decisions, especially when it came to Grymballia? "I just knew."

Lucy grabbed Rosie in the tightest hug and had tears in her eyes. "I was so scared for you."

"You're very brave, Rosie," Nathan said.

The warm cheeks returned. "Thanks."

They celebrated with a little dance and more hugs. Nathan and Rosie chatted about their exciting science project venture that was sure to win big awards, and they all felt confident that Miranda was no longer a threat.

"Should we tell our friends the good news?" Rosie grasped the acorn necklace.

They walked toward the cave to call Princess Nilly and Giblet.

Chapter 17

Rosie sat at the cave entrance and drew the castle's image in the dirt of the floor. She rubbed the acorn necklace, closed her eyes, and chanted the words to open the portal. She glanced to Nathan and Lucy and added, "Princess Nilly, it is safe. Please let us back into Grymballia."

The acorn glowed bright and filled the cave with light. The dark cave wall transformed into a swirling tunnel of light as the portal appeared.

Goblet hopped out of the portal and threw his arms around Rosie. "Thank you for getting my brother back, Rosie." He glanced around the cave quickly. "Is she gone?"

"She's gone, and she won't be bothering Grymballia any more." Rosie hugged Goblet tight.

Goblet stood tall and pointed to the portal. "Shall we?"

Nathan and Lucy wasted no time and leaped into the portal. Rosie nodded to Goblet and she stepped inside. The familiar whirling in her head and stomach forced her to close her eyes as she floated through space. The ride was soon over as she plopped onto the cave floor in Grymballia. Lucy helped her up and Goblet arrived minutes later.

They ran outside of the cave and Rosie rolled in the green grass. "I'm so happy to be here and know that Grymballia is safe." She kissed the dirt. The scent of flowers filled her nose and she knew that lilacs and rose bushes grew nearby. She turned onto her back and gazed into the blue sky as the sun warmed her face.

"Goblet, is it always summer in Grymballia?" Rosie realized the temperature had increased about ten degrees and it no longer looked like fall.

"It is a steady 65 – 75 degrees that is perfect for growing our crops, but we have the occasional rain to help things grow," Goblet said.

Lucy shook her head. "Must be nice! Do you or the Larmox have any huts in your village big enough for me to move into?"

The waterfall tumbled in the distance and Rosie hoped that her nightmares of a dead and dry Grymballia would never be seen again. A rainbow arched through the sky and songs flowed from the forest. Rosie warmed inside and felt safe, peaceful, and as if she was home.

Maddy burst off of a trail and bounded toward Rosie with Princess Nilly and Giblet close behind her. Nugget sprinted up and leaped into Rosie's arms and licked her face.

"Rosie!" Maddy screamed. "You're back!" Maddy had flowers woven into her hair and looked like a garden princess.

"We're back, and Grymballia should be safe." Rosie looked to Princess Nilly. "Miranda ate the peach."

Princess Nilly nodded with a proud smile. "We watched your actions in the Paradise Falls, Rosie. You saved us all."

Rosie shifted on her feet and dropped her head. "How's Spike? Does he remember Grymballia yet?"

Nobody spoke and Princess Nilly and Giblet exchanged an awkward glance.

Rosie wanted to know more but Maddy tugged on her shirt. "I got to see Giblet's house, Rosie. His mommy put flowers in my hair."

"You look so pretty, Maddy." Rosie watched as Princess Nilly and Giblet whispered to each other.

Princess Nilly turned to Rosie and the group. "You saved our world and have allowed all of us to live in peace with protection from the outside world. Come to the castle." The princess motioned and turned toward the trail. "We have something special planned for you.

Nathan replied as they walked. "We would do anything for you, Princess. Your world is special and we'll do our best to protect it."

"Ditto." Lucy pounded her fist in the air.

Rosie grasped her journal that she now had back from Miranda. "Princess Nilly, I'm sorry that my journal endangered Grymballia. I feel awful."

Princess Nilly stopped and turned to Rosie. "It's okay, Rosie, it was not your fault. We knew you were special, but today you risked your own future with Grymballia to protect us. We have a special celebration to honor your bravery. We can no longer see darkness in the Great Waterfall because you changed the future of Grymballia."

"Can we stay for the party, Rosie?" Maddy tugged on Rosie's arm and bounced up and down.

"Sure, sounds like fun."

Maddy squealed and clapped her hands. "Rosie, can I show you Giblet's house? I want to go there again and tell his mommy thank you for the pretty flowers in my hair."

Rosie looked to Giblet and he nodded his approval. Rosie realized it was hard to tell how old he was, because she was surprised that Giblet's mother lived at his village. She thought of Giblet as an old, wise soldier of Grymballia.

"Giblet, can I ask an embarrassing question?" Rosie gathered her nerve. "How old are you?"

Giblet smirked. "How old do you think I am?"

Rosie glanced to Nathan or Lucy for support. Lucy shrugged and Nathan flashed all of his fingers on both hands multiple times. "How about sixty-four?"

Giblet stopped walking and his naturally buggy eyes grew wide, and then he collapsed to the forest floor rolling in laughter. He giggled like a little girl and couldn't stop for a solid five minutes. Then his laughter triggered mass giggles in the group and it took a while for anyone to be able to speak.

Giblet eventually stood up and wiped the tears of laughter from his eyes. "I haven't laughed that hard since Goblet fell off of a Blim Bird into the swamp."

Goblet hollered, "Hey!"

Giblet looked to Rosie. "I'm a little older than you, Rosie. I turned fourteen last month."

What?

"No way!" Lucy stomped her foot. "But you are the portal master and the main man to Princess Nilly?"

He held his head high. "Yep."

Goblet wrapped his arm around Giblet. "He's worked hard to get to this position."

Rosie looked to Giblet in a whole new way. With respect. "Good for you, Giblet."

Princess Nilly interrupted. "You have a few minutes to visit Giblet's village, and I will return to the castle to finalize your party plans with the rest of your friends. We will see you soon." She zipped into the trees.

Maddy ran ahead with Nugget stopping to sniff every tree. Rosie walked with Giblet and Goblet and wanted to ask more questions now that Princess Nilly was gone. "What's going on with Spike? You guys are not telling me something. I feel awful he ate the magic peach in my bag."

Giblet did not look at Rosie. "We had a hard time at the portal getting Spike into Grymballia. He didn't understand, and it was like getting a porcupine into an elevator." Giblet shook his head. "When we got to Grymballia, he didn't recognize his brothers, Dennis and Rufus, and he hasn't spoken much to anyone since."

Rosie wanted to cry. Poor Spike, his life was ruined. "Can't the King reverse the spell?"

"No." Giblet whispered. "At least not that he knows of, but he's calling out to other counsels for advice as we speak."

Rosie stopped and fell to her knees with her head in her hands. "Oh, Spike! It's all my fault."

Giblet and Goblet squeezed her shoulder. "Spike can take care of himself. Maybe he shouldn't have sampled a taste of everything in your backpack?"

Maddy and Nugget circled back, and Maddy ran up to Rosie. "What's wrong? Why are you sad?"

Rosie stood up and dried her eyes. "I'm okay, Maddy." She didn't want to worry Maddy. "Where's Giblet's house?"

Giblet pointed to a dense patch of trees ahead. "We're almost there."

Giblet marched into the thickest part of the forest. He easily scooted under the ferns, bushes, trees, and overgrown grasses as a miniature Fimbalian, but Rosie and the rest of them could not see far in front of their faces. A green wall of plants surrounded them and it was easy to lose their direction.

"Is something going to jump out at us? I can't see anything but leaves in my face." Lucy pushed at tree branches and tripped on plants.

"Our village is hidden deep in the forest," Goblet replied.

Maddy maneuvered the underbrush easily since she was half the size of Rosie. She kept up with Giblet and plowed through the dense forest. Giblet whistled a tune as he hiked. The same tune echoed from the nearby forest.

Nathan tapped Rosie on the shoulder. "Did you hear that?"

Rosie nodded.

The whistling grew louder and the echoes flowed from many different directions. Giblet stopped. Ferns, bushes, and weeds surrounded them, but Rosie could not see a village anywhere. Giblet smacked his tail three times and said the words:

"*Appear, Appear, Bring It Near.*"

In front of their eyes, the wall of greenery lowered to the ground as if someone pulled the roots into the earth. A large circle clearing appeared. Maddy pointed at my stunned face. "I looked like that, too."

A pond filled the clearing and dozens of Fimbalians strolled around as green chubby bodies busied themselves in various activities. It was a village of Giblets! Friendly faces waved as Rosie and their group looked around. Lily pads covered the pond and upon these floating green leaves sat the Fimbalian houses. A hammock hung from twigs next to a small hut made of acorns, corn husks, and dried leaves cemented with the slime of the Larmox. The materials had to be light in order to float on the lily pads. As they walked by the pond, many Fimbalians were swinging in their hammocks with their skinny green legs crossed.

"Like I said before," Lucy said, "I'd move in here anytime."

Maddy said, "Rosie, this is where Giblet lives." She pulled Rosie toward the edge of the pond and the hut was the largest on the water.

"This is where Giblet and Goblet live, and their mommy lives over there." Maddy pointed and waved. "Hi, Giblet's mommy!"

Giblet's mom was an exact replica of Giblet, only she wore a pink dress and white apron, and her long nails and horns were all painted pink. She waved to them and her familiar wide toothless grin was outlined with lipstick.

"Welcome, Rosie. We're so honored to have you visit our village. Please make yourself at home." Giblet's mother radiated the same warmth as Giblet, and Rosie warmed inside to meet such a wonderful family.

"Giblet, your home is much bigger than the rest of the Fimbalians." Nathan noticed. "Why is that?"

"Since Goblet and I are the primary gate-keepers of Grymballia, we have special privileges. There's great risk with our job, so they gift us with a bigger home," he answered.

"You deserve it, Giblet, especially after what you suffered with Miranda." Rosie still felt guilty and pictured Giblet's tiny body strapped down and attached to wires. "You had to be so scared."

"My job is to protect Grymballia, and Miranda surprised me at the cave. But I knew you'd come." Giblet smiled.

"How were you able to leave us the acorn necklace, Giblet?" Nathan asked.

Giblet stuck out his chest with pride. "It wasn't easy." He held up his hand for emphasis. "When I realized it was not you guys at the cave, I leaped through the portal and closed it as soon as I could so she couldn't get into Grymballia. Miranda lunged for the portal opening, but tripped on the net.

She dropped the acorn necklace and I grabbed it before she noticed. As Miranda dragged me out of the cave, I hid the necklace in the rocks with a Dum-Dum that I knew my friend would recognize." Giblet grinned at Maddy.

"I found it right away, Giblet!"

"You saved everyone, Giblet," Rosie said.

Maddy tugged on Rosie's hand. "Rosie, look at Giblet's bed." Maddy ran to the water's edge.

Maddy reached toward his lily pad home, and Rosie noticed that Giblet's house contained miniature furniture as well as a hammock. Rows of cattails formed a soft, fuzzy bed and his pillow was a cluster of milkweed fluff. A small slide arched off the back of his hut and into the water so he could slip in for a swim whenever he wanted. Two tiny pots sat next to his bed.

"What's in the pots by your bed?" Lucy asked.

He rubbed his belly. "My sweets! We may not have candy in Grymballia, but we have honey. Goblet and I are lucky to have our own honey pots, and I sip some sweetness in the middle of the night to help me sleep."

Rosie realized she should have guessed it would be related to sugar. Throughout the Fimbalian village, Giblet's family and friends were friendly and welcoming. They offered honey and cabawocky fruit (a favorite food of the Fimbalians).

"We better get going to the castle." Rosie hated to leave such a warm place. "You are welcome to join us!"

Cheers erupted throughout the village.

Rosie, Nathan, Maddy, and Lucy left the village and Giblet escorted them to the castle. Maddy probably would not have left the village if Giblet did not join their group. The mood was light and, for once, they could enjoy Grymballia without having to hide, run, or save somebody. Rosie rubbed the golden acorn hanging around her neck and it felt warm as it glowed.

"Listen," Nathan said.

Everyone paused. The heavenly tunes of Grymballia floated across the warm air from all directions. They were close to the castle, and Rosie noticed the trail was different than she had ever seen it on previous trips.

Lucy noticed too. "Look at those flowers!"

Flowers bloomed up on each side of the trail towering over their heads, and green vines shot off the tops to form an arch over the trail. They walked under a blooming, scented canopy of flowers and vines. Rosie sketched in her journal the blissful scene. She was walking on air and looked down at her feet. Pink algae coated the trail with a soft cushion of carpet, and it lead directly toward the castle. Rosie felt like a princess.

Chapter 18

Rosie walked up the castle steps and was surprised by the silence.

"I thought there was a party here?" Lucy said.

Rosie shrugged. "This is where we're supposed to meet. Maybe Princess Nilly is inside?"

Nathan pulled open the grand doors of the castle, and Rosie's mouth dropped open with shock. The castle was packed with all of their Grymballian friends cheering and waving.

Rosie put her hands up to her face. "Oh, my gosh." She tried to hold back the tears of happiness to see all of her friends in one place.

"Woohooo! Now that's a party!" Lucy charged inside hooting and hollering.

A banner stretched across the front lobby that read: *OUR HEROES*. Tiny winged creatures in multiple colors filled the air dropping flower petals and helicopter seeds from maple trees. One of the winged creatures flew up to Rosie and landed in her outstretched palm.

Her petite fairy-like body was shimmery blue and she had aqua blue hair that flowed down to her feet and floated in the air like water. She wore a dress made of blue Forget-Me-Not flowers woven into a masterpiece of fashion. She bowed to Rosie and then zipped off into the air. She left a trail of blue glitter in the air.

Rosie couldn't speak. She glanced over to Nathan who had watched the whole scene and stood with his mouth gaping open. He said, "What was that?"

Giblet pointed to similar fairies in the air. "Flower Sprites. They are responsible for certain flowers in Grymballia and keep them growing, watered, fertilized, and happy."

"They're beautiful," Rosie watched them flit gracefully through the air.

Giblet grunted. "Don't let them fool you. A Flower Sprite has the sting of a wasp and could drop a Fligarian to his knees!"

Rosie put her hands on her hips. "Then why didn't they help us battle the Fligarian?"

Giblet rolled his eyes. "Exactly! The Flower Sprites are pretty, but only on the outside."

The King and Queen sat on their thrones smiling and clapping to the music as they looked around at their kingdom. Princess Nilly flew toward Rosie.

"Welcome to your party! This celebration is all in your honor. Grymballia's future looked bleak, but now you saved us from Miranda and we owe you our lives." Princess Nilly clasped her hands together and bowed her head toward Rosie.

Rosie didn't feel she deserved such praise. She shifted on her feet and her cheeks warmed. "I did what I had to for my friends." Rosie dropped her head.

"Come join the party." Princess Nilly motioned. "We have more surprises in store for you."

Nathan, Lucy, and Rosie looked at each other with uncertainty, apprehension, and a touch of excitement. Maddy had wondered off with Giblet, and Nugget tagged along likely trying to find Sid.

Rosie was watching the Flower Sprites overhead when she heard the music playing. The air was charged with energy.

As they neared the front of the castle lobby, the source of the jazzy music was revealed. Lucy jumped up and down and pointed. "They have a band!"

Sharp spikes shot out of Rufus and Dennis as they sat in front of coconut shells drumming a mean beat. Tiki sat in front of a table with six glasses of water filled to different levels. He used his love of water to create tunes as he tapped each glass. High-pitched tones echoed. Priscilla sang lead vocals. She grasped the microphone stand with all eight legs and her cherry red lips belted out deep, jazzy tunes as if she headlined in New Orleans. She wore a tight sequined gown and a tiara on her head. A diva at her finest.

Rosie looked around for Spike, but he was nowhere to be seen. Her stomach dropped. "Where's Spike? Why isn't he with his brothers?"

Nathan and Lucy surveyed the crowd and shook their heads. He was nowhere to be seen.

As they shuffled around the room, new faces stopped and said, "thank you" or "good job." Rosie felt like a movie star and wanted a quiet corner to hide for a while. Finally, familiar faces arrived as Sammy, Henry, and Jojo flew by with other Larmox.

"Sammy," Rosie yelled to get his attention. "Stop. Where are you going?"

"Oh, Rosie! We were just . . . we have to…" Sammy glanced to Jojo awkwardly.

"You guys are our heroes." Jojo gushed. "We would love to talk, but we have to take care of some Larmox business." She shoved Sammy to keep him moving.

Sammy and Henry nodded their heads rapidly in agreement and turned immediately to fly away.

Lucy tapped her foot in annoyance. "We just got ignored by flying worms."

"Something's up." Nathan looked around the room. "Where did everybody go?"

Rosie could not find Maddy or Nugget and the band no longer played. The King and Queen still sat on their throne talking to the Flower Sprites, but Princess Nilly, Giblet, and Goblet had disappeared.

Rosie approached the thrones. "Excuse me, but where did everybody go?"

The King's eyes twinkled and he reached up and twisted the pinecone at the top of his throne. "The party moved to Paradise Cove."

It seemed mysterious and weird that nobody told them about moving the party. Rosie glanced to Nathan and Lucy who hesitantly walked toward the tiny tunnel to Paradise Cove.

Rosie turned to the King and Queen. "Is Maddy down there?"

"Yes, she is," the Queen said. "Your presence in Grymballia is important to us. Never forget that."

Also, weird. Why would Rosie forget that? Was she going somewhere? "Thank you."

"We love it here," Lucy answered.

They were about to enter the tunnel when Rosie paused. "Excuse me, your Highnesses, but is Spike okay? Will he get his memory of Grymballia back?"

The King removed his crown and lifted off the throne and flew toward Rosie. "I'm afraid not. I can't find enough powerful magic to reverse the spell."

Rosie gasped. "What? You mean he will never remember Grymballia again? Where is he?"

The King flitted his wings and rested on Rosie's arm. "You did nothing wrong, Rosie. Spike is confused and trying to spike those he does not know. Right now we're holding him down below for safety, but he is comfortable."

"In the dungeon!" Lucy blurted.

The King nodded. "Yes, for now. Until we find a cure or he is safe to release and won't hurt anyone."

Rosie didn't care about a party and wanted to see Spike, but what could she do?

The small door behind the thrones glowed brightly, and the King motioned for them to walk that direction. Rosie ducked into the tunnel leading to Paradise Cove.

She immediately smelled the water and the earth hidden down below, and she heard the rumble of the Great Waterfall churning the pool below it.

"I wonder when we'll come back here again?" Lucy asked without looking up.

"I don't know," Nathan responded. "I feel awful about Spike."

"Wouldn't it be great if we could come and go whenever we wanted and never have to worry about anyone finding out. We could see our friends all the time." Rosie knew that couldn't work. They had been very careful, but Miranda threatened to destroy Grymballia and Spike got hurt. Rosie dreaded leaving again.

At the bottom of the stairs, lush green landscape stretched out toward the waterfall, but nobody was in sight.

"Why is everyone being so mysterious?" Rosie asked. She looked over her shoulder and the King and Queen did not follow them into the tunnel.

"Maybe they're under the falls in Paradise Cove?" Nathan shrugged. "But I don't know how we get in there because Princess Nilly always did it before."

They walked toward the falls and the sun glowed bright overhead. Flowers covered the landscape with colorful blooms and sweet scents. The fine mist of the waterfall showered Rosie's face.

Rosie dipped her toe in the water and the cold swirling current felt good after a long day of adventures. A partial rainbow formed in the spray of the waterfall as it caught the sunlight. She heard a bark.

"Nugget!" She whipped around and knew it was Nugget's bark. It came from behind some trees.

Nugget bounded toward her and leaped into her arms, followed by a parade of their Grymballian friends. An actual parade!

Leading the parade, Maddy wore a wreath of beautiful flowers on her head and a long robe covered with orange and yellow blossoms. She held her head high as she marched with a staff in her hand, but she glanced over to Rosie and waved furiously. "Hi, Rosie!"

Nugget's collar was adorned with yellow flowers and she sprinted back to the parade to walk next to Sid. Sid's pink curls were fluffed up like a pom-pom ball and her teeth were polished white. Princess Nilly flew overhead and her leaves changed colors from orange to red to yellow and back to orange again.

Princess Nilly waved to Rosie. "Welcome! We have a special ceremony in your honor. Your friends are all here." Princess Nilly glowed.

Giblet and Goblet walked side by side with their chests puffed out and chins up. The horns on their head and on their tails were polished and tipped with gold. They wore vests covered with gemstones. Rosie tried not to giggle because their vests barely fit over their chubby bellies that jiggled as they walked.

"Look at them!" Lucy pointed to Kimmie and Lila. "I want to do that!"

They slithered along side by side, and their skin was tattooed with colorful designs. Images portrayed the sun, rainbows, Nugget, a Fligarian, and a girl holding a peach.

"That's me!" Rosie pointed. Their tattoos told the story of their time in Grymballia.

Tiki waddled up next. He was wearing a fancy hat made of clam shells that he gathered from the lake where he lived. He played a small flute with water bubbling a tune as he bobbed his head to the melody.

The Larmox followed Tiki in the best parade Rosie had ever seen, and Sammy flew in front with his green wings beating steady. He tipped his bright purple top hat and nodded to Rosie. Henry hovered lower to the ground due to his larger body and whistled a snappy tune. Jojo flew back and forth wild with excitement and waved to everyone as she blew kisses.

Suddenly, a web shot toward Rosie and stuck to a tree. Priscilla launched through the air and landed on the web. "Hello, darling," she said. Every leg had pink ribbons attached that streamed behind her as she flew. Priscilla busied herself crafting the word HERO into her web. She then shot it again and disappeared into the distance with pink ribbons flapping.

Nathan sat on the grass. "This is unreal. They did this all for you, Rosie."

Rosie turned her head abruptly. "Not just me, but for all of us. I couldn't have done it without all of you guys."

Lucy added, "Rosie, admit it, you're the queen of this beehive. We're just the worker bees."

Rosie grunted. "That's ridiculous."

The Glaperians were next in the parade and Xena led with her brilliant blue wings, magnificent eyes, and furry body. She was followed by her sisters; Trina - a bright green, Dina - a brilliant yellow, and Nina - a deep red, and Gina - purple. Patsy's jet black wings and body followed a short distance back to distinguish her differences. As they flew by Rosie, the Glaperians spun in a dance that blended their colors into a mesmerizing display.

Rufus and Dennis walked by, and everyone knew that something (or someone) was missing. They lacked their usual spunk but still kept their heads held high as they marched with their boots and swords. They paused and tapped their swords on the ground three times, and their spikes shot out in every direction. They bowed to Rosie and continued walking.

Rosie imagined Spike sitting in a cell in the dark, cold dungeon where they had rescued Nugget. She watched Rufus and Dennis march away without their brother.

She had to think of a way to get Spike's memory back.

The parade ended with the Blim Birds. Three of them walked in front of Rosie, Nathan, and Lucy, and then they knelt down for them to hop onto their backs. They launched into the air flapping their enormous wings to soar inside Paradise Cove. They disappeared in and out of the rainbows made by the Great Waterfall. Rosie scratched the cat-like ears of her Blim Bird as she tipped her face into the wind. After diving, gliding, and soaring through the sky, they returned to the party below and gently returned to the grass.

"My friends, please sit down." Princess Nilly held her hands in the air and motioned for them to join the others seated in a circle. "To thank you for your kindness, bravery, and saving

Grymballia more than once, we have something special for you."

Rosie glanced at the others and they returned nervous glances. Maddy sat next to Giblet and Nugget. Rosie picked at her fingernail and noticed the other Grymballians stared at her with excitement.

Princess Nilly pointed to Nathan. "Nathan, for your intelligence and technical abilities, I present you this." She held out a brown leather bag.

Nathan slowly stood up and grasped the small bag, but stared at it with a furrowed brow. "What is it?"

"It's a magic bag – the Inquisitor's Pouch. If you need the answer to something you don't know, all you have to do is ask, and then reach into the bag. The answer will be inside."

Nathan cupped the bag in his hand like a fragile kitten.

Princess Nilly continued. "It can only be used three times per trip to Grymballia, but you can also take it home and use it there. With each return trip to Grymballia, you will be allowed three more questions."

Nathan stared at the pouch. "Thank you, Princess Nilly. This is a very generous gift." Nathan almost stumbled as he sat back down. He glanced to Rosie with big eyes.

"What are you going to ask it?" Lucy elbowed him. "Are aliens real? Is Lucy the most awesome person ever? Or maybe . . . will dinosaurs rise again?"

Nathan shook his head. "No. I'm not asking it any of those questions." He sat quietly and Rosie wished she knew the thoughts and questions racing through his head.

Princess Nilly pointed to Lucy next. "Lucy, for your loyalty and brutal honesty, we have a special gift for you. You can be a Grymballian for a day." Princess Nilly grinned at Lucy.

"I'm not sure I understand." Lucy stood up. "Do you mean I can use magic? Or that I can see through walls like Xena?"

"Yes, whatever you choose. You could choose a Grymballian power or choose to cast a particular magic spell. You can fly like Jojo or sling a web like Priscilla. Anything you wish."

Lucy's mouth hung open and Rosie could see the wild look in her eyes as she thought of the possibilities.

Princess Nilly then said, "The power you choose today will be your power whenever you return to Grymballia."

"What! I get it back whenever I come here?" She turned to Rosie. "Can you believe this? How can I choose?" She looked to all the Grymballians sitting in the grass.

Priscilla spun a web into the shape of star, Tiki sat at the water's edge using his flippers to churn up bubbles and tiny fish, Henry burrowed under the crowd so he could get a better look of Nathan's Inquisitor's Pouch. The Glaperian's hovered overhead beating their wings and scanning with their eyes.

Lucy looked up toward the rays of sun shining through the opening of Paradise Cove. She turned to Princess Nilly. "I know what I want."

"Anything."

"I want to fly."

Princess Nilly closed her eyes and nodded. "As you wish."

The room erupted in cheers as Princess Nilly waved her hands over Lucy and glitter filled the air. Lucy disappeared briefly, but after the glitter settled, a new Lucy came into view. Yellow incandescent wings had sprouted from Lucy's back, and she wore a gold sequined dress and shoes. Her wings fluttered and their sheen reflected the sunlight. Lucy squealed.

"OH – MY – GOSH!! I have wings!" She jumped up and down and then caught sight of her fancy shoes. "And these shoes! Princess Nilly, I love it."

Giggles spread through the crowd.

Nathan said, "Let's see what you can do."

A slight look of panic crossed Lucy's face. She glanced to Princess Nilly. "Can I really fly? Will I fall?"

"You can fly." She pointed to the sky. "Take off and your friends will guide you."

Patsy and Jojo flitted up next to Lucy, "Come on, Lucy. We'll help you. Flap your wings to get the feel of it."

Lucy took a few steps and frantically flapped her shiny yellow wings. As she squealed with delight, Lucy lifted into the air and hovered low across the ground.

"I'm flying! I'm flying, Rosie!" When Lucy waved and yelled, she lost her balance and tilted and almost crashed into a tree. "Whoa!"

Patsy and Jojo zipped to her side to steady her, and Lucy regained her balance. She flew higher into the air again. She soon became more comfortable, and floated on her new wings with ease.

Rosie and Nathan watched in awe. "I can't believe that's Lucy up there," Nathan said. "Did you ever think something like this could ever happen to us?"

Rosie turned to Nathan. "Never. We're so lucky. We may have to drag Lucy out of Grymballia by the wings. She's never going to want to leave."

Lucy glided in the clouds as if she had flown for a lifetime. She stretched out her arms, flapped her wings three times, and then floated while smiling into the wind. She soared across the treetops and skimmed the top of the Great Waterfall. The Blim Birds flew with Lucy through the rainbows, but while the Blim Birds disappeared, Lucy's golden wisps could still be seen. And her screams of delight could likely be heard in outer space.

Lucy struggled with her landing as she barrel-rolled onto the green grass and landed at Rosie's feet. As she lay on her back looking up at Rosie, she said, "I'm the happiest person on Earth." As she talked, her wings beat faster. She hopped to her feet.

"You looked great, Lucy," Nathan said. "You look like a real Grymballian up there."

"What did it feel like?" Rosie couldn't help but feel a tad jealous. Flying! Wow, that had to be amazing.

"Oh, my gosh. At first my stomach dropped to my toes and I felt like I was falling, but then I took a deep breath and – AAAH. It was so peaceful to have the breeze blowing my face and floating on air." Lucy closed her eyes as she relived her moments in the sky.

Jojo and Patsy landed next to Lucy. Jojo said, "Pretty cool, huh. You're never going to walk in Grymballia again if you can fly!"

"No way. Its all air time for me now." Lucy glanced to Rosie. "Well, maybe not ALL the time."

"Can I touch your wing?" Rosie couldn't resist examining the shimmering, thin wing with so much power.

"Of course!" Lucy turned around so her wings faced Rosie. Nathan stepped up to examine them also.

Rosie reached out hesitantly because the wings looked paper thin and delicate. She caressed the edge and it was soft and velvety, but warm because it was part of Lucy.

"That tickles!" Lucy giggled.

Rosie could see fine ridges and the golden, shimmery pattern covered an underlying tough thick material that only appeared delicate. "This feels as thick as leather!"

Nathan nodded. "How is it sheer and transparent when it is so tough? What is this made of?" He looked to Princess Nilly.

Princess Nilly flew closer. "The Sippi Wasp produces a sap that becomes thick like glue. It has many uses in Grymballia to avoid plastics and other non-biodegradable options."

"Wow. I wish we had Sippi Wasps." Rosie thought of all the possibilities to avoid plastic bottles, containers, and packed landfills.

"Rosie," the princess grinned. "It's time for our next surprise."

"There's more?" Rosie couldn't believe that anything could top Lucy flying through the air.

The Grymballians and everyone gathered back in a circle next to the waterfall. Rosie sat next to Lucy, but had to leave more room for her wings. Princess Nilly waved her arms to get attention.

"Another person we need to thank for saving Grymballia is . . . Maddy."

Maddy gasped and threw her hands to her face. "Me?"

Tiki and Priscilla yelled out, "Yay, Maddy!" and Sammy, the Larmox, threw his hat in the air in celebration.

The princess continued, "You helped rescue Giblet and have been kind and gentle. You deserve our gratitude."

"What does that mean?" Maddy whispered to Rosie.

Princess Nilly grinned. "That means we want to thank you for being Giblet's friend, and we want to give you a present."

"Oh! I know what that means!" Maddy sat up on her heels and clapped her hands together.

Princess Nilly flitted close to Maddy so they were face to face. "Maddy, would you like to be a Fimbalian while you are in Grymballia? We could transform you into the same shape and size as Giblet, so that you can explore and play in his village while you're in Grymballia."

"I could be like Giblet?" Her eyes grew wide and she looked to Giblet with sheer excitement and joy. "Yes! Yes, yes, yes!" She jumped up and down.

Princess Nilly raised her hands to cast the spell, but Maddy's face dropped. "Wait." She held up her hands. "Will I stay that way forever? Will it hurt?"

Rosie's could barely speak and had many questions of her own. How can she take care of her sister . . . as a Fimbalian? What if she gets stuck that way? Not sure Maddy could go to second grade looking like Giblet.

Princess Nilly grinned. "It will not hurt, and it will only last while you're in Grymballia. Afterward, you will return to normal Maddy."

Rosie stepped forward. "Princess Nilly, as a concerned big sister, is there any risk of her staying a Flimbalian? I'm not sure what Mom and Dad would say if I brought home a shorter, green sister."

"I promise, Miss Rosie, your sister will turn back to her true self without harm."

"Thank you, Princess Nilly." Rosie felt better. A little.

"Okay, Maddy, are you ready?" The princess raised her arms with a twinkle in her eye.

Maddy stood next to Giblet and held his hand. "Giblet, I get to be like you!" She bounced on her toes and closed her eyes. "I'm ready."

Giblet looked worried, and that worried Rosie. He was protective of Maddy and Rosie knew he didn't want her to get hurt. The Princess waved her arms and sparkles filled the air as a tornado of glitter surrounded Maddy. Rosie lost site of Maddy in the whirlwind.

She gasped. "Where'd she go?"

When the cloud cleared, Maddy was gone.

Wait a minute. . . Maddy was there, but in a smaller, greener version. She stood eight inches tall and still held Giblet's hand. She was a lighter shade of green than Giblet and looked slimy, but Rosie recognized her eyes.

Maddy, the Fimbalian held her skinny green hand in front of her face and her eyes grew wide. She opened her mouth wide (and Rosie was thrilled to see that she still had a mouthful of her own teeth) and she screamed. "I'm green!"

She twirled in a circle as if she were wearing a fancy skirt and admired her new skin. She had a small patch of curly hair on top of her green head with three horns jutting through. She flipped her horned tail, and her blue eyes sparked. "Rosie, I look beautiful!"

Rosie wasn't sure what to say. Beautiful was not the first word to come to her mind, but Maddy was happy. "Yes, you are Maddy."

Maddy hugged Giblet and for the first time she didn't have to kneel down or bend over, and she was not afraid to squish him. She wrapped her arms around him tight and squeezed. "You're my best friend, Giblet."

"You make a fine Fimbalian," Giblet said.

Maddy did another spin but mid twirl, she caught her foot on her tail, and fell onto her face. "Ouch!" She rubbed her nose. "I'm not used to having a tail."

Giblet helped Maddy up off of the ground, and then he pounded his tail on the ground. Sparks flew and hundreds of butterflies swirled around Maddy and then fluttered into the sky. He said, "You'll get used to your tail, and may even learn a few tricks."

"Whoa! Can I do that too?" Maddy thumped her tail in the dirt and only a small puff of smoke fizzled.

Goblet patted her on the shoulder. "It takes practice. We can teach you a few tricks."

"Rosie, can I go to Giblet's village and learn magic?" Maddy pleaded and the Fimbalian's blue eyes were still her beloved sisters underneath the green. "Please, please, please. I want to jump on lily pads and swing in Giblet's hammock."

Rosie glanced to Giblet and Goblet. "Are you sure about this? She may want to stay Fimbalian forever." Rosie trusted Giblet and knew she was in good hands, but the uncertainty of how long she would be green made her uneasy.

Giblet waved his hand at Rosie. "Or she may realize how good she has it in her world!"

Rosie knelt down to Maddy. "Go and have a great time with Giblet and Goblet. We'll come get you when it is time to go home."

Maddy reached her arms out for a hug and Rosie picked her up. Maddy stood on her hand and appeared like a toy action figure. "Thank you, Rosie."

Rosie leaned forward and Maddy wrapped her arms around Rosie's face and her hands only reached to Rosie's ears. Rosie sat Maddy back onto the forest floor and she sprinted off with Giblet and Goblet toward their village. She turned to wave at Rosie, tripped on her horned tail, and then hopped up and took off running again out of Paradise Cove.

Off to one side, Rufus and Dennis stood alone. Rosie ached inside for their brother, Spike, and wanted him back to normal. A rumble of chatter grew louder and Rosie saw Sammy and Henry pointing at her, while Tiki and Kimmie whispered while looking her direction. What was going on?

Rosie soon found out what all the whispers were about. Princess Nilly yelled to the crowd. "I need your attention! It's time to present Rosie with her gift."

Cheers erupted.

Chapter 19

Everyone settled back on the grass and Rosie picked nervously at her fingernail. She didn't like being the center of attention.

Lucy's wings buzzed. "What do you think you're surprise will be? Maybe we can fly together!"

Rosie squirmed on the grass. "I don't need anything. I wish Spike was back to normal, but if they could do that, I'm sure they would've already."

Princess Nilly quieted the group.

"Rosie, you have been essential to saving Grymballia. You led the team against the Plyrim soldiers, you were fearless against Miranda, and you risked your own memories of Grymballia to save us."

Rosie dropped her head and couldn't look at Princess Nilly. Her face flushed. Nathan elbowed her, "You deserve every minute."

Princess Nilly continued, "You are now considered an honorary Princess of Grymballia. My sister in spirit - Princess Rosie."

As she finished her sentence, Trina and Dina flew toward Rosie carrying a lavish robe covered with daisies, roses, and orchids with wisps of ferns shooting out to make it a plush garment. The back of the robe had a brilliant sun representing Grymballia. Trina and Dina rested the robe on Rosie's shoulders and she breathed in the sweet aroma of flowers.

"I-I-I can't believe this." Rosie was shocked. She looked into the excited eyes of the cheering Grymballians and tears filled her eyes. She did not feel this special even when she earned her Girl Scout recycling badge or her spelling bee trophy. "I don't know what to say. A princess? How can I be a princess?"

Princess Nilly flitted over to Rosie and landed on her shoulder. She kissed Rosie a tiny peck on her cheek and said, "A princess leads her people to safety, protects them from danger, and makes difficult decisions for her people. You ARE a princess, Rosie."

Lucy flew into the air and twirled in an aerial spin as she chanted, "Princess Rosie! Princess Rosie!"

The rest of the Grymballians followed with their chants. Tiki, the Larmox, the Glaperians, and Lila and Kimmie screamed out her name, and Priscilla weaved *Princess Rosie* into a web.

Princess Nilly explained, "As our honorary princess, Rosie, you share a leadership role in Grymballia, and anyone may come to you for advice or help. With princess responsibilities come magical powers. While you wear the robe, you have powers only in Grymballia, but not in the outside world. We know you will use this power wisely."

Rosie looked to Nathan and his eyes were huge. Magical powers?

Lucy screamed, "Whoa, Rosie! You could turn Nathan into a frog."

"Lucy!" Nathan yelled.

Lucy fluttered over to Nathan. "She wouldn't turn you into a frog." Lucy grinned as she hovered in front of Nathan buzzing her wings. "But maybe a salamander?"

Rosie waved her hand to Lucy. "I would never do that, Nathan." She turned to Princess Nilly. "Thank you, Princess Nilly, but I have no clue how to use magical powers. What if I accidentally start a fire or glue Lucy's mouth shut forever."

Nathan laughed. Rosie honestly worried that she might hurt someone. She glanced down at her magical hands. The special robe carried not only the weight of its flowers and greenery, but new responsibility.

Princess Nilly spoke softly and in a reassuring tone. She seemed to sense Rosie's nerves. "The magic will come naturally. If you want something to happen, you imagine it in your head, and then it will occur."

She made magic sound so easy. Rosie tried to clear her mind and not think about anything specific. She didn't want to cause something to happen accidentally.

"I almost forgot!" Princess Nilly turned toward Rufus and Dennis walking toward Rosie carrying a tiara.

Rosie bent forward and they placed it on her head. The tiara was a delicate green crown of woven grasses and wildflowers. Rufus and Dennis bowed at her knees. Rosie should feel like a princess, but she felt guilty.

"Princess Nilly, can I use my power to get Spike's memory back?"

Rufus and Dennis immediately turned toward Princess Nilly with hope in their eyes.

"I'm so sorry, Rosie. Even the King is unable to help Spike."

Rosie dropped her head as Rufus and Dennis rolled off to join the other Grymballians. She touched the tiara on her head. "Princess Nilly, I am so honored by all of this and will treat my role as princess with great respect."

"I know you will, Rosie. We have one last thing to give you," Princess Nilly said.

From behind the Great Waterfall, Kimmie and Lila slithered forward balancing something on their backs. It looked like a glass ball. Kimmie beamed as she reached Rosie's feet. "I'm so excited for you, Princess Rosie."

"Oh, Kimmie, that sounds crazy! Princess Rosie? That will take a while to get used to. But I couldn't have done any of it without you and all of my team." Rosie looked around to all of her friends.

Kimmie and Lila rolled the glass ball off of their back and Rosie picked it up.

Princess Nilly explained. "This is the Magical Eye of Grymballia. When you return home, you can gaze into the Magical Eye and see Grymballia at any time."

Rosie cupped it in her hands and cradled it like a precious gem. She could see Grymballia whenever she wanted! She looked up and forgot that Maddy was off running around with Giblet as a little green monster, she would be so excited to see the Magical Eye.

Nathan walked up to Rosie. "Wow, that will be so cool to be able to see everyone when we're home."

The possibilities raced through Rosie's head. "You mean I'll be able to see you all whenever I want, and see rainbows and waterfalls and Franklin and Blim Birds and all my friends?" Rosie's voice grew loud and screeching with excitement.

"Yes." Princess Nilly said.

"I love it!" She held the Magical Eye close to her chest. "I love this more than being a princess, because I will never have to be far away from you all. Thank you, thank you."

"You're welcome, Princess Rosie." Princess Nilly nodded. "Okay, everyone, let's celebrate! We have fruit and juices and entertainment."

Everyone jumped up and cheered. Friends darted in many directions and Rosie was mobbed with hugs. She gripped her Magical Eye and pulled her robe tight around her shoulders. She took a deep breath, in and out, relishing her friendships and Grymballia. Lucy flew circles in the air and Nathan held tightly to his Inquisitor's Pouch of answers.

"This has been the most amazing day. I can't believe what we've been given." Nathan said.

"I know, right?" Rosie said. "We're so lucky."

Lucy zipped up to Rosie and Nathan. "I'm going to fly by the Great Waterfall."

"Be careful, you're still getting used to your wings." Nathan warned.

Lucy darted off. "Since I can only fly in Grymballia, I'm using these wings as much as possible." She took off into the sky.

Lucy floated toward the mist and rainbows of the Great Waterfall and rarely wavered, she had become accustomed to her wings quickly. As she neared the tumbling water of the falls, a swift breeze shot up and caught one of her wings. She tumbled end over end and dove straight toward the boulders below.

"Lucy!" Rosie screamed and ran to the water's edge. She closed her eyes and wished that Lucy wouldn't crash.

Suddenly a red beam of light shot from Rosie's hands toward Lucy. It wrapped Lucy's falling body in a bubble of safety and she stopped tumbling. Lucy regained her balance and flew straight again and hurried away from the waterfall.

Rosie's hands shook and she couldn't move.

"Did you do that?" Nathan stared at Rosie.

"I – I'm not sure," Rosie said, "but I think so."

Lucy landed in front of Rosie with her face pale and her arms wrapped around her chest. "You saved me, Rosie."

"How do you know it was, Rosie?" Nathan asked.

"I could feel her all around me," Lucy gazed back toward the waterfall with glassy eyes. "I was falling and I couldn't move, but I felt Rosie's arms catch me."

Rosie shivered. She had performed magic. "Whoa."

Lucy threw her arms around Rosie with her wings flapping. "Thank you. I'd be a squished bug on those rocks if you hadn't saved me."

Music played around them and everyone celebrated.

Tiki waddled up to them. "Princess Rosie, I'm so excited to call you that." Tiki said.

"Tiki, I'm not sure I'm ready to hear the word princess yet."

"It sounds perfect." He smiled.

"Your music is beautiful, Tiki," Lucy said. "You didn't tell us you were such a musician."

"I love music. My whole family plays music at our lake. We use the water in every instrument we play." He held his head high with pride.

Jojo and Patsy flew toward them giggling. Their friendship had blossomed into a tight bond between Glaperian and Larmox. Jojo said, "Princess Rosie, let's go visit your little green sister, Maddy."

Rosie clapped her hands. "What a great idea! I can't wait to see Maddy in Giblet's village. I bet she's having the best time ever." Rosie held up the Magical Eye. "And I have so much to tell her."

Rosie, Nathan, and Lucy announced they were headed to the Fimbalian village with Patsy and Jojo, and others wanted to join. Sid wanted to see Nugget since they would have to leave Grymballia soon. Kimmie and Priscilla also came along.

Rosie couldn't imagine leaving Grymballia again. She gripped the Magical Eye and knew it would help to keep them close, even when far away. Before leaving Paradise Cove, Rosie gazed at the Great Waterfall and rainbows. The Grymballians that were not joining them waved frantically. "Good-bye, Princess Nilly, come back soon!"

Chapter 20

As they left the castle and hiked toward Giblet's village, the sun warmed their crew. Rosie was sweating in the heavy robe, but she didn't want to be disrespectful and take it off. Lucy flew overhead with Patsy and Jojo, and Priscilla hitched a ride on Sid's back.

"Rosie, you should see the view up here. I can see all the way to the cave," Lucy yelled from above the treetops.

"Wow, that must be amazing." Rosie tried to picture flying with her own wings and to see the same view as when riding on a Blim Bird. *If only she could fly.*

Red light flashed and Rosie's insides flipped. She wobbled on her feet and her head spun. Her feet lifted off of the ground.

"What's happening?" Rosie grabbed at Nathan but she floated away.

"Rosie, you're flying!"

The ground drifted away with Rosie pawing at the air for balance, but it didn't help. Her heart raced, she kicked her feet at the air, she flapped her arms, but then she took a deep breath and tried to relax. She had wished she could fly – and now she drifted in the breeze with cool air blowing her hair. Amazing.

On the ground below, Nugget barked and Sid waved. Nathan whooped and hollered and Priscilla yelled, "You did it, darling!"

Lucy noticed Rosie in the air and almost fell out of the sky with surprise. Lucy darted toward her. "Rosie, how are you flying?"

Rosie spread her arms out to her side for balance and finally flew straight. "Well, I should be careful what I wish for."

Lucy flew circles around Rosie. "It pays to be a magical princess."

"Let's fly, my friend." Rosie quickly gathered her courage and flying skills, and they zipped forward to the clouds.

Flying through the clouds caused tiny water droplets to collect on Rosie's cheeks, and it felt wonderful. Flying on her own was different than flying on a Blim Bird, because she controlled every turn, lift, speed, and direction she wanted. If she chose to fly under Franklin's canopy – she did. If she chose to soar over top of a rainbow – she didn't hesitate. "I honestly feel like a magical princess," Rosie said to Lucy.

"How can we possibly sit in Mr. Hack's class again after flying through clouds?"

"No kidding." Rosie soaked up the beautiful view and couldn't bear to think about Mr. Hack's class or returning home. On the far borders of Grymballia, Rosie saw mountaintops and a far away land that she never knew existed. A clear border of Grymballia was evident by rows of dense black trees, but beyond the land appeared beautiful. There were no mountains in the forest of Rosie's world, but they were present inside the magical landscape of Grymballia. She pointed, "Lucy, what do you think lives out there?"

Lucy squinted. "Wow, I never noticed that. I don't know."

"There's such a black border between Grymballia and the mountainous land, I wonder why?"

Rosie wondered why Princess Nilly never mentioned it. Down below, Nathan motioned that Giblet's village was close. Rosie and Lucy glided down to the trail. Rosie decided to walk to visit Maddy. A red flash and seconds later, Rosie could no longer fly and her feet were firmly set on the ground.

"Glad to have you back," Nathan said. "How was your flight?"

"Magical," Rosie answered.

Rosie heard the familiar Fimbalian whistles and knew they were close to Maddy and the Fimbalian village. They walked into the thick brush and headed toward the pond. They stopped.

"How can we get inside the village without a Fimbalian?" Nathan asked.

Priscilla waved her glittery boot as she lounged on the back of Sid, nestled in her pink fur. "A princess can get into any village." She winked at Rosie.

"I can?" Rosie was not sure she liked all the power that came with her princess position. It made her nervous.

Everyone turned toward Rosie waiting for her to act. She closed her eyes and tried to remember the chant Giblet spoke to reveal the hidden village. Her eyes popped open and she

raised her arm to a wall of grasses and bushes.
"*Appear, Appear, Bring It Near!*"

A red beam shot into the air as the wall of green parted to reveal the Fimbalian Village. The Fimbalians erupted with cheers to greet their arrival.

Rosie scanned the huts and lily pads for Maddy, but had a hard time picking her out from the other green Fimbalians roaming around. She walked toward Giblet's house at the edge of the pond and Maddy's giggles carried across the water to greet Rosie.

As she walked up to Giblet's house, Rosie wished she had a camera. A Fimbalian with blonde curls stretched out swinging in Giblet's hammock, while Giblet's chubby belly poked up as he lounged on his cattail bed. Both of their hands were buried in the honey pot and honey dripped down their chins.

"Hey, Maddy! Looks like you're having fun," Rosie yelled.

"Rosie, you're here!" Maddy tried to leap out of the hammock, but got stuck and rolled out like a seal. She eventually bounced on a lily pad over to where Rosie stood. "I'm having the best time ever! You look funny, Rosie. What's that fancy coat?"

Rosie glanced down at her robe. "It's a robe that Princess Nilly gave to me. You're all sticky! Do you like life as a Fimbalian?"

"It 's the best ever, and we need to tell Mom and Dad to buy honey. I love it!" Maddy took off running toward the edge of Giblet's hut and leaped onto the slide. "Watch, Rosie!" She slid down the maple leaves and dove into the water as she squealed the entire way.

Maddy disappeared into the pond and didn't come back up. Rosie's stomach dropped, but then Maddy's horns popped up and she shot water into the air like a fountain from her mouth. Giblet jumped off of his bed and flew down the slide and splashed in the water with Maddy.

"At least you're washing all the honey off." Rosie yelled.

They eventually returned to shore and Nathan and Lucy came to join them in the grass. Maddy was dripping wet, but ran up to Rosie for a big hug.

Maddy chatted frantically. "Rosie, I have to show you what Giblet taught me."

Giblet took two steps backward. Rosie decided to follow his lead and also stepped back. Maddy scrunched up her face in concentration and lifted her horned tail.

"Ready? Here I go!" Maddy smacked her tail on the ground three times. A small puff of smoke surrounded her, but nothing else happened.

Lucy giggled. "You can make smoke bombs! Cool."

Maddy stomped her foot. "Giblet, it didn't work!"

Giblet said calmly, "Try it again."

Maddy took a deep breath, closed her eyes, and slapped her tail three times.

Sparks flew and surrounded Maddy, and when they cleared she held something in her arms. Rosie gasped.

Nathan leaned forward. "What is that?"

Maddy beamed with pride. "A doll!" She held up the tiny Fimbalian doll she had magically produced that wore a frilly dress with pigtails. "I made it with my own magic!"

Rosie nodded and couldn't help but smile. "That's great Maddy. You've learned a lot already."

"Can I keep the doll?"

"Sure, but we'll have to come up with an explanation for Mom and Dad."

Maddy danced around with her new green doll. Rosie wondered what Baby Annabelle and Tilly would think of the newest member at the tea party.

"Why are you dressed like that, Rosie?" Maddy asked as she stared at Rosie's robe.

"Princess Nilly made me a princess. This is a special robe that I wear whenever we're in Grymballia, and it gives me magic powers." Rosie waited for the screams . . .

. . . and soon they echoed off the water. "Oh, my gosh, Rosie! You're a princess?"

"Only in Grymballia, but I have another surprise." Rosie showed Maddy the Magical Eye. "When we're at home, we can look into this ball and see our friends in Grymballia."

"Whenever we want?"

"Whenever we want." Rosie replied.

Maddy jumped across lily pads. "Giblet, we can talk all the time! It will be like Skype!" She sat next to Giblet on a lily pad with their legs dangling into the water.

Lucy whispered to Rosie. "Maddy looks cute green. How are you going to tell her we have to go home now?"

"I know. She's having so much fun that I hate to spoil it." She turned to Lucy. "Isn't it going to be hard for you to leave and not be able to fly to school?"

Lucy lifted off her feet and fluttered her wings. "It's going to be awful."

Rosie knew she had to break the news to Maddy, but also wanted to be sure she was not green forever. "Maddy, we have to go home now. Mom and Dad are going to wonder where we are soon."

Her head dropped and she stopped splashing the water with her foot. "Now?"

"Yes." Rosie said. "And we need to change you back to the normal Maddy again."

Kimmie slid up next to Rosie. "You can change her back, Princess Rosie. Your power can do many things."

"Really? I can change my sister back to a human? That doesn't sound like a good idea." Rosie looked at Maddy - tiny, innocent, and green. "What if I do something wrong?"

"You can do it, Rosie," Kimmie said. "We have confidence in you."

Maddy wrapped her arms around Giblet and hugged him. "I had so much fun today, Giblet. This was the best day ever."

Giblet patted her horns. "When you come back to Grymballia, you can become a Fimbalian again if you wish. The decision is yours."

179

"Yes, yes, yes!" Maddy clapped her hands. "I want to be Fimbalian every day!" This seemed to help Maddy get ready to change back to herself knowing that she could be green again someday soon. "Will you keep this for me until I come back?" She handed Giblet her new Fimbalian doll.

Giblet nodded and pulled the doll to his chest.

Rosie's hands were sweating and she felt nauseated. "Are you ready, Maddy?"

"I'm ready." Maddy stood before Rosie at knee level and looked up with her big blue eyes.

"I'm nervous, Maddy. I don't want to make a mistake." Rosie knew she had to think hard about what she wanted to happen and it would occur. She kept worrying about messing up and turning her sister into a puddle of purple slime.

Red light glared and Rosie shielded her eyes.

Maddy glowed with red light and began to change shape.

"No!" Rosie yelled. "Wait! I wasn't ready. That's not what I meant!"

Maddy melted into a purple puddle of slime with blue eyes and a mouth.

Rosie dropped to her knees. "Maddy, what did I do?"

The eyes in the slime shifted, and then it spoke. "Rosie? What's wrong?"

Rosie shot a look to Lucy and Nathan. *HELP ME.*

Nathan ran to her side. "It's okay, Maddy. Rosie can fix it. Right, Rosie?"

Rosie's lip quivered. "I made a mistake, Maddy."

"Why?" The Maddy slime-puddle jiggled and her eyes grew bigger. "What happened?"

"I turned you into - slime. I'm SOOO sorry." Rosie put her hands on her head and pulled on her hair. "I was thinking in my head what I did NOT want to happen, and then it happened." Rosie shook her head. "I can't believe I did this, but I'll fix it." She wished Princess Nilly were here to help or maybe the King and Queen. How could she do this to her sister?

"Hurry, Rosie. I don't want to be slime." Maddy was now a crying puddle of purple slime.

Rosie concentrated. She blocked out everything including the rustle of the trees and the birds singing. She tried to think about Maddy playing in her bedroom at home, but her mind kept returning to purple slime with blinking eyes.

"I can't do it!" Rosie squeezed her fists.

Maddy wailed. Giblet tried to comfort the Maddy slime but his fingers got stuck and covered with purple goo.

Lucy stood face to face with Rosie and put her hands on her shoulders. "Rosie, listen to me. You were chosen as a princess for a reason. You are a leader and we trust you. Maddy needs you. You can do this."

Rosie nodded her head and took a deep breath. Maddy needed her. Rosie closed her eyes and pictured Maddy standing in front of her with blonde curls, blue eyes, and holding a Dum-Dum. She wanted her sister back in her normal form.

The red lights returned, swirled around her, and then hovered over the purple slime. The slime pulsated and then grew bigger as it changed shape. Slowly the figure of Maddy developed and stood in front of Rosie.

Rosie threw her arms around her sister. "Maddy, I'm so sorry."

"You did it, Rosie." Maddy squeezed tight. "I'm not sure I'll ever play with slime again."

Giblet nodded to Rosie. "Congratulations, Princess Rosie. You're performing powerful magic."

They journeyed to the cave dragging their feet and in no hurry to return home to their own world. Lucy took a few last laps in the sky before she would lose her wings for a while. Rosie stayed on the ground and walked with her Grymballian friends to enjoy their company a while longer.

Lucy landed by the cave and her yellow glittery wings relaxed against her back. "I'm sure going to miss flying."

Nathan rubbed his pouch and stared into the Grymballia valley.

"Have you thought of any questions to ask?" Rosie nudged Nathan. "I'm not sure I could only pick three."

Nathan looked worried with his eyebrows furrowed and lips pursed. "I have an idea." He looked around to see who might be listening. "What if I asked the Inquisitor's Pouch a question about Spike?"

"Yes! What a great idea." Rosie got incredibly excited.

"What are you waiting for?" Lucy bounced up and down and pointed to Nathan's magic pouch. "Ask!"

Nathan held the Inquisitor's Pouch in front of him and glanced from Rosie to Lucy. "Here it goes," he said. He closed his eyes and held the bag high. "Inquisitor's Pouch, will Spike get his memory back?"

Silence.

Nathan opened his eyes and turned to Rosie. She shrugged. Lucy said, "Maybe this bag is a dud, and you need to get a new one from Princess Nilly."

Sparks erupted from the bag, and Nathan almost dropped it for fear of getting burned.

The sparks died down and the pouch sat quiet.

"Now what?" Rosie asked.

Nathan pulled the bag closer. "Princess Nilly said I have to reach into the bag for the answers."

"Heck no!" Lucy shouted. "You could get your hand burned off, how do you know it won't shoot fire again?"

Nathan peered into the bag. "I think it's okay." He reached his hand inside.

Rosie watched his face change from apprehension and fear to curiosity and then to excitement. "There's something in here!" He pulled an object out of the bag.

Rosie leaned in closer. "What is it?"

"A piece of paper." He unfolded it and read it out loud. "It says: *YES*."

They screamed.

"Spike will get his memory back! We have to tell the others." Rosie was thrilled, but paused. "But wait, we still don't know how to get Spike's memory back?"

Nathan stared at the pouch.

"Do it." Lucy whispered.

Nathan asked, "How can Spike get back his memory of Grymballia?"

They waited for what seemed an eternity.

Sparks erupted and after they died down, Nathan reached into the bag.

Rosie leaned forward. "What does it say?"

He read the paper. "*Zalenda Tree, Deviland.*"

"What the heck does that mean?" Lucy threw her hands in the air. "What good is a magic answer if it's in a language we don't understand?"

Giblet broke into the middle of our circle. "What did you just say?" He looked directly at Nathan with a grave look on his face.

"When? Just now?" Nathan showed Giblet the piece of paper. "I asked the Inquisitor's Pouch how we could get Spike's memory back."

Giblet paled and grabbed Rosie's leg for support. She had never seen Giblet falter. "What is it, Giblet? What does it mean?"

Giblet blinked slowly and then looked up. "Deviland is another civilization beyond our borders."

Rosie chimed in. "Is it the one beyond the black border? I saw it when I was flying! It looks beautiful."

Giblet shook his head. "Beauty cannot hide the evil that lives there. Our King and Queen charmed the forest to protect Grymballia from the Deviland people."

"Then why would the pouch direct us there?"

Giblet only shook his head.

A noise erupted from the forest. Princess Nilly charged through the trees and flew directly toward them. "Wait! Wait! Don't leave yet." She screamed as she flew.

Breathless and exhausted, Princess Nilly could barely speak. "I'm so happy I caught you before you left."

"What is it, Princess Nilly? Is everything okay?" Rosie asked.

"It's fantastic! The King found a possible cure for Spike's memory."

"That's great! How?"

"The fruit of the Zalenda tree will cure him. We just need to find where one is grown, and we can return Spike to normal." Princess Nilly clapped her hands to her chest.

Rosie almost fainted and Nathan groaned. Giblet sat down in the dirt, and Lucy said, "Well that's perfect."

Princess Nilly's face fell and she looked confused.

Nathan showed Princess Nilly the piece of paper from the Inquisitor's Pouch. *Zalenda Tree, Deviland.*

The princess gasped. "No! Not Deviland."

Giblet calmed down Princess Nilly. "We need to return to the castle to plan our strategy."

Princess Nilly squeezed Giblet's hand and looked into his eyes. "But Giblet, Deviland?"

They flew off together leaving Rosie standing dumbfounded as they disappeared into the forest. Spike could be cured, but Grymballia was up against an unknown evil - again. If Rosie didn't get home soon, their parents could make it feel like an unknown evil when they were grounded for days.

"We have to get home," Rosie said. She turned toward the cave.

"But how can we leave them?" Lucy pointed toward the castle. "Spike needs our help and Deviland does not sound like a trip to the Caribbean."

Rosie glanced at Maddy. "I know, but we have to get home safely first and talk about our options." Rosie couldn't risk Maddy getting hurt.

They walked into the cave just as Giblet rushed back in behind them. "I almost forgot that you couldn't get home without me!" He drew the pattern in the cave floor and the portal glowed in the wall. He chanted:

Land of the Earth, we must leave you now,
We keep all your secrets, we solemnly vow.
Nature's our friend and we will never neglect
Grymballia we now leave and always protect.

Good-byes were said filled with tears and emotions. It got harder every time. Nugget and Sid sniffed and nuzzled. Priscilla, Kimmie, Patsy and

Jojo blew kisses and wrapped them in hugs. Nathan and Lucy grabbed Nugget and slid through the portal toward home. Rosie peeled Maddy's arms off of Giblet as she clung and reminded her that she could see him soon in the Magical Eye. Maddy said good-bye and they inched toward the portal.

Before sliding back home, Rosie squeezed Giblet's hand and looked deep in his eyes. "Can Spike be saved?" she asked.

Giblet faltered and dropped his eyes. "Deviland is our worst enemy. It will not be easy."

Rosie knew that Grymballia would never give up on Spike. She looked into Giblet's eyes and said, "We'll be back to help."

Giblet looked up with shock – and hope. He squeezed Rosie's hand before she disappeared into the portal.

Chapter 21

As they landed in the cave, Rosie noticed she no longer wore a robe or tiara. She was no longer a princess. Lucy patted her back missing her golden wings. They filed out into the late day sun and headed for the trail.

They relived their day as they hiked, and couldn't believe how much they had packed into one day. Lucy had flown with real wings, Maddy was a Fimbalian, Nathan had the answers to any question at his fingertips (and still had one question left in his pouch), and Rosie was an honorary princess of Grymballia.

And their powers returned every time they visited Grymballia.

"We absolutely cannot talk about Grymballia at school." Nathan warned. "Miranda almost destroyed their whole world and we can't risk that happening again."

Rosie knew it was true and she pulled her journal out of her backpack. She flipped through the pages and looked at sketches of Giblet and Priscilla and the songs she had heard from the forest.

She had to hide her journal.

"I have an idea." Rosie stopped in the trail. "We need to hide my journal in a place that only we know about. We'll keep the information about Grymballia in case we need it for some reason, but protect it so nobody can steal it from my locker or backpack."

"Good idea," Lucy said. "Where should we hide it?"

Maddy kicked the dirt. "Why not here?"

Rosie nodded her head. "Maddy's right! We all know this trail better than anyone. We can bury it in a safe place that we all agree upon."

"Perfect." Nathan looked up and down the trail. "Do you guys know that tree with the crazy twisted trunk and big knots sticking out all over?"

"Yes!" Everyone yelled in unison and pointed down the trail. They sprinted toward the location.

The knotted, twisted tree stood at the edge of the trail with its leaves turned red for fall. Together they dug a hole between two roots. Rosie wrapped her journal in a plastic bag, and tucked it into the hole.

"It will be safe here." Rosie stood up and felt as if she were leaving a part of herself behind.

They continued hiking and were almost home. Rosie sighed.

Nathan heard her and said, "What an adventure. Saving Grymballia from Miranda, each of getting special gifts from Princess Nilly, and then discovering our friends are about to journey into another dangerous situation. Its quite a lot for one day."

Rosie recalled Spike riding in her backpack, and the images of the peaches haunted her brain. She felt responsible and needed to help Spike. Dennis and Rufus needed their brother back, and Spike was a great soldier for Grymballia. Rosie said, "I want to help them get the fruit of the Zalenda tree in Deviland."

Nugget barked to punctuate the sentence with an exclamation point. Lucy and Nathan didn't hesitate. "I'm in."

Maddy waved her hand. "Me too!"

Rosie started to plan their next adventure.

Epilogue

School resumed with Lucy and Rosie passing notes in Mr. Hack's class and a new science fair project combining Nathan, Rosie, and Miranda's genius to create the most fantastic project ever. Miranda never spoke of Grymballia, and Rosie and Lucy ate lunch with her occasionally.

Every night before bed, Maddy tiptoed into Rosie's room and they curled up on Rosie's pillow with the Magical Eye. They called to their friends and talked to Giblet, Tiki, Princess Nilly, Priscilla, Sammy, and all their friends whenever possible. Nugget also hopped onto the bed and barked at Sid.

The nightmares stopped, and Rosie enjoyed sweet dreams of Grymballia.

I stepped out of the cave wearing a crown and my royal robe. Grymballia's blue skies forced me to shade my eyes as I watched the Blim Birds fly overhead darting in and out of rainbows. I walked down the path toward the castle and raised my hands. Red light shot out and I flew over the treetops easily until I landed on the castle steps. Princess Nilly greeted me, Welcome home, Princess Rosie."

Home. Before joining my friends in the castle, I enjoyed the comfort of Grymballia. I stood gazing at the birds and the wispy clouds overhead as I smelled the flowers all around. In the distance, at the boundaries of Grymballia, a thunderhead of black clouds was building like a fortress in the sky.

Storms were coming.

Acknowledgments

Thank you to my family and friends for their never-ending support, proof-reading eyes, and an end of the day beverage when needed.

Thank you to my patients for supporting my love of writing, because I know sometimes I'm not there when needed.

Thank you Connie Heckert and Jill Esbaum for endless support and guidance.

Check out my website:

www.patmccawauthor.com

COMING SOON

JOURNEY TO DEVILAND

Book three and the final installment of the Grymballia Series.

Made in the USA
Columbia, SC
17 January 2019